AMPHIBIANS' END

END

A KULIPARI NOVEL

BY TREVOR PRYCE WITH JOEL NAFTALI

ILLUSTRATED BY SANFORD GREENE

AMULET BOOKS

NEW YORK

AMPHIBIANS' END

A KULIPARI NOVEL

Library of Congress Cataloging–in–Publication Data

Pryce, Trevor, author.
Amphibians' end : a Kulipari novel / by Trevor Pryce, with
Joel Naftali ; illustrated by Sanford Greene.
pages cm
Summary: The Spider Queen is dead, but the powerful scorpion
Lord Marmoo and his fearsome army are still a threat to the Amphibilands,
especially as the Rainbow Serpent has told the frogs that they must lower the veil
that protects them—so the young wood frog Darel and his friends must search the
Outback for answers in the quest to bring peace and water to their land.
ISBN 978-1-4197-1648-5 (alk. paper)
1. Frogs—Juvenile fiction. 2. Scorpions—Juvenile fiction.
3. Animals—Juvenile fiction. 4. Magic—Juvenile fiction.
5. Water—Juvenile fiction. [1. Frogs—Fiction. 2. Scorpions—Fiction.
3. Animals—Fiction. 4. Magic—Fiction. 5. Water—Fiction. 6. Fantasy.]
I. Naftali, Joel, author. II. Greene, Sanford, illustrator. III. Title.
PZ7.P9493496Am 2015
[Fic]—dc23
2015004203

Printed and bound in China
10 9 8 7 6 5 4 3 2 1

Amulet Books are available at special discounts when purchased in
quantity for premiums and promotions as well as fundraising or
educational use. Special editions can also be created to specification.
For details, contact specialsales@abramsbooks.com or the address below.

ABRAMS
THE ART OF BOOKS SINCE 1949
115 West 18th Street
New York, NY 10011
www.abramsbooks.com

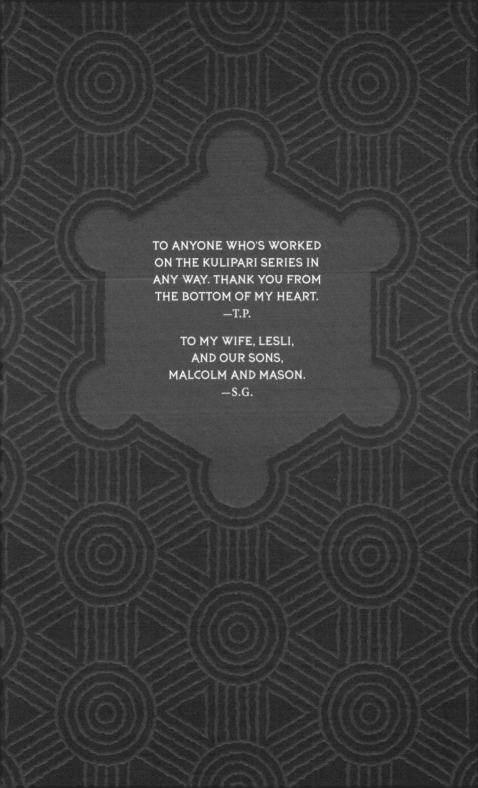

TO ANYONE WHO'S WORKED
ON THE KULIPARI SERIES IN
ANY WAY. THANK YOU FROM
THE BOTTOM OF MY HEART.
—T.P.

TO MY WIFE, LESLI,
AND OUR SONS,
MALCOLM AND MASON.
—S.G.

POSSUM VILLAGE

TRAPDOOR
SPIDER VILLAGE

TO THE
AMPHIBILANDS

THE OUTBACK

N
W E
S

GECKO VILLAGE

THE RED ROCK
TOWER

MAP OF THE
DESERT
AND SURROUNDINGS

DAREL

GURNUGAN (GEE)
DAREL'S BEST FRIEND

DAREL'S MOTHER
A WOOD FROG

GEE'S MOTHER
AND FATHER

ARABANOO
A TREE FROG

THUMA   THARTA

DAREL'S YOUNGER
TRIPLET SIBLINGS

COORAH

COORAH'S
FATHER

TIPI

ARABANOO'S
GANG

A HEALER

DAREL'S FRIEND AND
AN APPRENTICE HEALER

FROGS AND PLATYPUSES

LORD MARMOO
LEADER OF THE SCORPIONS

COMMANDER PIGO

PARALYSIS
TICKS

LORD MARMOO'S
SECOND-IN-COMMAND

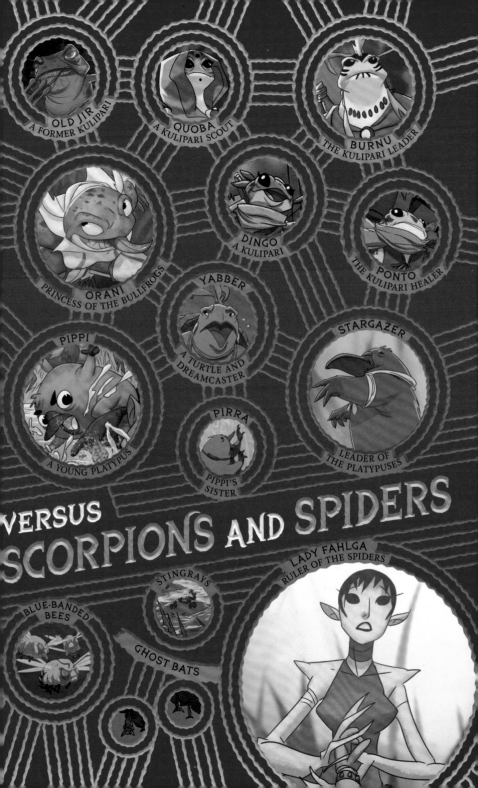

1

OMMANDER PIGO SKITTERED BESIDE
Lord Marmoo as they trekked through
the outback toward the Amphibilands. His main eyes scanned the
darkness for threats, but his side eyes
kept drifting toward Lord Marmoo's
face.

Toward Lord Marmoo's *ruined* face, scarred from
the frog chief's attack.

Pigo had to admit that he almost admired the
frog's cunning. Even after the spider queen's magic
had made his lordship nearly invincible, the frog still
managed to trick Lord Marmoo into swallowing the
burning pepperbush.

Now Lord Marmoo's mouthparts were twisted, his
jaw was half-melted, and two of his side eyes were a
cloudy white. He looked more like a nightmare than
a warrior. He seemed to be losing his mind, too, but
Pigo didn't say anything—a scorpion always obeyed his
commander.

So while Lord Marmoo ranted in the darkness,
Pigo just murmured, "Yes, my lord" and "Of course,
your lordship."

"They think they've won?" Lord Marmoo said
now, slashing a bush with his pincers. "They haven't
won . . ."

"No, my lord."

"I don't need an army." He gestured to the empty hillside behind him. "I *am* an army. I don't need a spider to tear down the Veil. All I need is a rip large enough for me to enter . . . And that much still remains."

"Yes, Lord Marmoo."

They approached the peak of the first of the Outback Hills, and a damp breeze washed away the harsh scent of desert. Pigo's mouth watered, and Lord Marmoo made a hungry noise in his throat.

"Recognize this?" Lord Marmoo asked when they came to a rocky outcropping with only a few trees.

Pigo looked at a boulder and then at the branches of a crooked tree. "This is where the spider queen wove her web."

"And beyond is where the frogs defeated us," Lord Marmoo said, an edge of hatred in his voice.

"The Kulipari are strong, Lord Marmoo. They're a powerful enemy—"

"They are *nothing*! They're pond scum! It's that pathetic, mud-stinking grub Darel, who's defeated me twice now. This time, I will crush him in my pincers."

"Yes, m'lord."

Lord Marmoo gestured in front of them toward the moonlit hillside. "And the path is still open, the Veil is still torn. I'll have him soon."

"But the frogs have been building defenses for weeks."

"Nothing can defend against *me*," Lord Marmoo snarled.

The faint ribbiting of sleepy frog guards sounded in the darkness, and Pigo gazed toward the sound and saw the tear in the Veil. A wide, jagged shape like a cave mouth opened among the shrubs on the hilltop, and the night seemed sharper and more vivid beyond. When Pigo looked through it, he saw moist, leafy foliage in the moonlight—as well as sharpened logs, lined up like fence posts, and tangle-vines draping across branches.

Lord Marmoo stalked forward, through the tear and into the Amphibilands itself, and Pigo followed dutifully along. The croaking stopped when the frog guards spotted his lordship—then Lord Marmoo smashed a sharpened log in half with a swipe of one pincer.

Frogs gasped and shouted, and a dozen dark shapes sprang at Lord Marmoo—bullfrogs in reed armor, swinging curved swords. "For the Amphibilands!" a female shouted. "For the—"

Lord Marmoo smashed her with a pincer, then knocked the others away with swipes of his segmented tail. "Throw yourselves at me, croakers, and I'll tear you apart! Or hide and I'll hunt you down. Those are your only two choices."

"I hate to be disagreeable," a mellow voice said in the dark night. "Especially on such a lovely evening. I mean to say, with the moon glowing and the owls hooting—"

"Yabber!" Lord Marmoo roared. "Show yourself!"

Torches burst into flame in the darkness, revealing Yabber, the long-necked turtle dreamcaster. He peered at Marmoo and said, "The pepperbush has left its mark. I'll try to heal you, Marmoo, if you stop all this—"

With a growl, Marmoo sprang toward Yabber. Tangle-vines whipped at him from the trees, entangling his legs and tail and pincers—but Marmoo simply flexed his carapace, unconcerned. A dozen tree frogs shot at him from the cover of trees, holding the other ends of the vines.

Lord Marmoo's stinger flicked and his pincers flashed. "You should thank me for such easy deaths! I had plans for you that aren't so kind as my stinger."

"Plans change," Yabber said, and his eyes started glowing golden.

"No dreamcasting!" Marmoo bellowed.

He leaped at Yabber over a hole full of burrowing frogs, snapping the vines entwined around his legs and tail. The frogs' spearheads sparked against Lord Marmoo's underbelly, but couldn't pierce his carapace as he sprang closer to the turtle.

Yabber's eyes suddenly glowed brighter, and the air shimmered with a rainbow sheen. A swell of power thrummed through the night and blasted Lord Marmoo backward, past Pigo. A moment later, the dreamcast explosion hit Pigo, shoving him through the tear.

He landed on four knees, with his other legs splayed, and stood unsteadily. "M-m-my lord!" he stammered, dizzy and disoriented. "He's fixing the Veil . . ."

The turtle's voice echoed from all around. "What is torn apart can be woven back together."

Pigo shifted all his eyes toward the turtle, but he couldn't see him. The frogs were gone, too. Completely vanished. The pointed spikes, the dangling vines—even the scent of torch smoke was gone.

"He did it," Pigo gasped. "He closed the tear."

For a long moment, Marmoo stared into the darkness, his eyes glinting with madness. Then he spun and marched past Pigo, toward the outback.

"The spiders tore the Veil once," he snapped. "They can do it again."

"But Queen Jarrah is dead," Pigo said, his voice soft. He knew better than to mention that Lord Marmoo himself had killed her.

"So they need a new queen." A tattered sneer spread across Marmoo's face. "Or a king."

2

EVERY FROG IN THE AMPHIBILANDS gathered at Emerald Pond for Chief Olba's funeral. The branches of the trees bowed under the weight of tree frogs, while burrowing frogs clustered on a mossy hill and bullfrogs watched from the shallows.

They all croaked together, a song of love and loss. Instead of standing with the wood frogs crowding the banks, Darel found himself sitting between Quoba and Burnu, their backs against the trunk of a banyan tree. To Darel's surprise, Quoba sang slightly off-key, and Burnu had a deep, resonant singing croak.

When the song faded, Darel asked Quoba, "How are you feeling?"

"Better," she said with a quick smile.

He didn't completely believe her. She'd drawn on her full power to defend the platypuses from Lord Marmoo—maybe even *more* than her full power—and ever since then, she'd been afraid to tap her poison.

Afraid that using any more of it would burn her out completely.

But he knew she didn't like talking about it, so he turned to Burnu. "How about you?"

After a taipan snake bit Burnu in a cave in the Snowy Mountains, he'd spent days weak and feverish. But now he nudged Darel and scoffed, "At my worst, I'm still better than a mud frog."

"At least your personality is back to normal," Darel said.

Burnu nudged Darel again, almost knocking him over. "Why aren't you off somewhere, tearing down the Veil?"

"Because there's a funeral going on," Darel said with a glare.

"And?"

"And there's something else we need to do before we lower the Veil."

Burnu snorted. "But you don't know what it is."

"Nope," Darel said, shaking his head.

"And that's why you told the loquacious reptile to repair the rip Jarrah made in the Outback Hills? Because it's not time yet?"

Darel didn't know what "loquacious" meant, but he nodded. "Yeah. At first I wasn't sure if he should bother, but I think . . . I think we need to keep the Veil strong until the right time."

"Do you really think there's a *right* time to leave the entire Amphibilands defenseless? When's the right time to let the scorps destroy everything you love?"

"I don't know." Darel toed the ground. "But this isn't only about us frogs. This is about the entire outback, about the future for everyone. This is about the Rainbow Serpent and—"

The raspy note of a didgeridoo interrupted Darel.

The crowd hushed as Ponto and Dingo pushed a raft into the water. The raft was mounded high with lily pads and lotus flowers, and dotted with leaf-bowls containing Chief Olba's favorite foods: honey snails and lice cream, fish eggs, and all kinds of grub.

Darel felt the hot prick of tears in his eyes as he watched the raft spin in the current, knowing that soon it would drift down the stream that flowed to the ocean.

After a moment of silence, a bullfrog hunter stood up and told a story about Chief Olba. Then Gee's father did the same. Frog after frog stood, sharing memories, and Darel was surprised by how many of the stories were funny. He hadn't expected all this laughter, mixed with the tears.

Finally, Old Jir limped forward and leaned on his cane. "Chief Olba loved three things. Food, laughter, and—"

"More food!" someone croaked.

Old Jir smiled, then lifted his cane, to indicate the frogs and the Amphibilands. "And all of this, all of *you*. She'd be proud that we remember her with songs and laughter. She lived to guide us . . . and she died to protect us."

The crowd hushed.

"But this isn't only the end of a life, it's also the beginning of a new day. The chief knew that." Old Jir looked across the pond. "And she's not the only one."

"King Sergu knew it, too," Yabber said. He'd quietly lumbered in to stand behind Ponto.

"And they both trusted one young frog to guide us." Old Jir's pale gaze shifted to Darel. "Darel, why don't you say a few words?"

What? No way. Darel felt his toe pads clench, and his stomach twisted in nervousness. "I—I'm not—"

Quoba prodded him with her elbow. "Stand up."

"Why don't *you* stand up?" he grumbled.

Burnu kneed him in the butt.

"Ow!" he yelped, hopping to his feet. Then he

raised his voice. "I mean, *how*, um, how nice to be asked." He thought for a second. How could he put into words everything he felt about the chief's sacrifice? "I just want to say that I miss the chief. I'd give anything to hear her voice again. Even if she was just scolding me for destroying the market-place. But . . . she's gone."

"And you want to tear down the Veil!" someone croaked.

"*I* don't want to," Darel said, his face flushing. "The *Rainbow Serpent* wants us to."

"So you say! What if you're wrong?"

"I . . ." Darel swallowed. "I saw the Serpent on the mountaintop. And then again outside the platypus village, after the chief sacrificed herself to beat Marmoo. The Stargazer showed me a rainbow on the river—and that's when I knew. That's when the Serpent told me, *Lower the Veil*."

"Why?" a Baw Baw asked.

"I don't know. Maybe because we need to face our enemy once and for all. Maybe we need to stop hiding and rejoin the outback. Maybe . . . I'm not sure. All I know is, we have to have faith."

Darel ducked his head. For a moment, he heard crickets. Then a few tongues thwapped, and silence fell, except for a soft crunching. Darel sighed. He didn't know what to say, but he knew he couldn't twiddle his finger pads any longer. He couldn't wait around, hoping that he'd suddenly understand everything the Rainbow Serpent wanted.

"We need a chorus," Darel announced. "We need to decide this *together*, all of us."

Old Jir raised his walking stick. "Chief Olba always loved a sing-along. I can't think of a better way to honor her than to have one last chorus, to decide if we lower the Veil."

A chorus was a village vote. The tree frogs peeped and the bullfrogs trumpeted, the wood frogs croaked and the Baw Baws rasped—they would sing and sing until they finally joined together in a single refrain, agreeing on a single decision.

"We've faced dark times before," Jir continued. "We were hunted almost to extinction before the Hidingwar. But in the end, the Serpent never let us down."

Darel took a breath. "So let's hear both sides of this question." He gave what he hoped was a wry smile. "Well, we all know why tearing down the Veil is a terrible idea."

"Because without it, the scorps will tear us

apart," a bullfrog rumbled. "Marmoo will kill us all."

"The Rainbow Serpent will protect us," another frog said.

"What's the Serpent going to do?" a tree frog peeped. "Dazzle the enemy with pretty colors?"

Other frogs muttered around the pond: *That young wood frog knows what he's doing*, and *He fought them off once already*, and *If we listen to him, we will lose the Amphibilands.*

A glow washed over Darel from behind: Burnu's colors shining brightly. Then the Kulipari leader's voice echoed across the pond. "If not for Darel, there would *be* no Amphibilands, not anymore."

"The chief trusted Darel," Quoba said, putting her hand on Darel's shoulder. "The turtle king trusted Darel. And the *Kulipari* trust Darel."

"Chief Olba chose Darel to keep us safe," Old Jir said, watching the flower-laden raft float in the pond. "That's good enough for me."

"Thanks," Darel said. "But it has to be good enough for all of us."

"Then tell all of us why we should lower the Veil," Coorah called.

"There's only one reason," Darel admitted. "And

that's because we have faith in the Rainbow Serpent. Because even though this is scary—terrifying, even—and dangerous, we trust the ancient spirit who brought life to the outback." He straightened, and looked at the crowd. "Maybe . . . maybe the choice isn't between staying safe and risking everything."

"Of course it is!" someone croaked.

"Maybe we're not safe inside the Veil," Darel continued, shaking his head. "Maybe Marmoo will find another way inside. Maybe he's already weakening the Veil. Maybe if we try to hide behind it, thinking we're safe, he'll catch us by surprise, totally undefended. We don't know. All we can do is trust the Serpent."

When he stopped speaking, a hush fell over the crowd. Then Old Jir said, "Those are our options! Do we trust the Rainbow Serpent and lower the Veil? Or do we keep the Veil and stay hidden?"

"Keep the Veil!" a burrowing frog called.

"Stay hidden!" a tree frog peeped.

"We think of the tadpoles," a wood frog croaked, "and we stay in the Veil."

Dozens of frogs joined the chorus, and a loud refrain of "Stay safe, stay hidden" echoed across the pond. Darel croaked, "Trust the Serpent," and heard the Kulipari joining in with him. He almost smiled when he saw his mother singing "Trust and faith." Gee and Coorah sang, "Lower the Veil," and Arabanoo and his tree frogs sang along in the branches, in surprisingly sweet voices.

"Stay safe" drowned them out, though. In a few moments, almost all the frogs were chanting together: "Stay safe, stay hidden. Stay safe, stay hidden."

The chorus grew louder as a breeze swirled through the trees and rippled the surface of the pond. The flower-strewn raft spun slowly, and the wind lifted flower petals in the air. They floated and twirled, then scattered across the pond.

As Darel croaked, "Trust the Serpent," he watched the petals tumble from the raft—and his breath caught in awe. The petals drifted into a pattern on the water: red and orange together, then yellow and green and blue and purple . . .

Like a rainbow.

The wind blew again, and the petals floated apart. The pattern disappeared, but Darel lifted his chin and sang louder. "Trust the Serpent, trust the Serpent . . ."

Slowly but steadily, the tide turned. The calls

of "Stay hidden" faded, and his mother's song of "Trust and faith" attracted more and more singers. A few minutes later, a single song rang out from Emerald Pond.

"Trust and faith . . ."

Now Darel just had to earn that trust. If he was wrong, he'd endangered everything he loved.

3

OLLOWING THE FUNERAL FEAST, YABBER headed off alone. He needed to think after watching the frogs' vote to lower the Veil. He agreed with the decision— trust came first—but he'd seen the Rainbow Serpent with his own eyes, while the village frogs relied on nothing but faith.

That impressed him, but it also scared him a little. King Sergu's death had left Yabber responsible for protecting the frogs with dreamcasting. But with the Veil down, he wasn't sure if he could. He lowered himself onto the riverbank, trying to force his stubby legs into lotus position.

"*Ooooooom,*" he breathed, closing his eyes. "I am the lotus, and the lotus is me. My shell unfurls like the petals of the flower—"

He meditated for a long time before he heard the patter of frog feet approaching. He cracked one eye and watched Darel flop down into lotus position

beside him. Of course it was easy for a wood frog—
they were mostly leg anyway.

"I can see you peeking at me," Darel said.

Yabber closed his eye. "I'm not peeking. I'm
attaining inner peace."

"How long is it going to take?" Darel asked.

"To attain inner peace?"

"To tear down the Veil!"

Yabber opened his eyes. "'Tear down the Veil.' It sounds easy when it's just a bunch of words, like 'Tickle a shark' or 'Lick the moon,' but how am I supposed to undo King Sergu's greatest casting? I'll admit I was his star pupil, but—"

"How long, Yabber?"

Yabber sighed. "Unraveling the Veil will take time and preparation."

"How much time and preparation?"

"And I don't think I can do it alone."

"Who else do you need?"

"Plus, the whole thing is . . . uncertain."

Darel frowned. "What does *that* mean? 'Uncertain'?"

"The Veil is big and complex . . ." Yabber scratched his neck thoughtfully. "Imagine you're chopping down a tree. It takes a long time to chop, but the tree will fall—*whooom!*—in the blink of an eye."

"How long before that happens with the Veil?"

"There's no way to know. At least a week, I would think, perhaps more."

"And then *whooom*," Darel said.

"Very *whooom*," Yabber agreed.

Darel sighed. "Then you'd better start chopping."

"Are we ready?"

"The Rainbow Serpent didn't say, 'Tear down the Veil whenever you're ready.'" Darel rubbed his face. "It said, 'Tear down the Veil.'"

Yabber exhaled softly. "Start now?"

"Start now," Darel said.

4

SWIMMING WITH THE RIVER CURRENT, Darel spread his arms and pushed the triplets forward on a gentle wave. They hooted and giggled, and paddled clumsily with stubby legs. They were relearning how to swim, now that they'd begun their transformations from legless tadpoles into froglings.

Darel slitted his nostrils in amusement. Sure, the entire Amphibilands was going to collapse at any moment, but at least the triplets still made him smile.

Then Tipi completely forgot how to use her legs, and started wagging her butt, trying to scoot forward. Tharta bobbed along like a floating twig, swirling and dipping. Only Thuma was making any progress—except in the wrong direction.

Darel sloshed them around a turn in the river. "Use your legs! Slow and steady! Pull them toward your belly and—"

"Platypuses!" Thuma squealed.

Darel glanced downstream, where a row of creek oaks rose over the river and dozens of inviting holes—platypus burrows—lined the muddy riverbank. Furry brown platypuses flashed through the water, while more floated on the surface. A few older platypuses built furniture on the top of the riverbank, and a handful of young ones dug rocks from a steep strip of dirt beside the burrows.

Darel grinned. The young ones were making a mudslide.

The other two triplets turned. "They're everywhere!" Tipi said, her eyes bulging.

"Look at their tails!" Tharta flopped his own tail, which still hadn't completely disappeared, trying to whack the water like a platypus.

"I heard the boys have poison like us," Thuma said, gaping at all the activity.

"You don't have to be a boy to have poison," Tipi said indignantly.

"That's true," Darel told her. "Look at you, the mightiest Kulipinki."

Tipi was the smallest of the triplets, but Darel suspected that one day she'd become the most powerful. She glowed a bright pink when she got upset or excited, and she was already strong enough to lift Darel over her head—which made bedtime a challenge.

"You need to be a boy to have poison if you're a platypus," Thuma insisted.

"Who needs poison anyway?" Darel asked.

Tipi splashed him. "Easy for you to say."

"You've got other talents," Thuma said.

"Like talking to the Rainbow Serpent," Tharta added.

"And being the Blue Sky King," Gee said, splashing into the river.

"Gee!" the triplets cried, tumbling through the water toward him. "Did you bring candy?"

"Darel's not a blue *anything*," Thuma said as Gee handed out snacks.

"I'm also not a sky anything," Darel said. "Or a king anything. It's just a dumb nickname."

"I don't get it, either," Gee admitted, munching on a honey worm. "I also don't get"—he licked his frog fingers—"why platypus honey is so much better than frog honey."

"'Cause we're *that* sweet," Pippi said, her face poking up from the water beside him.

The triplets stared at her with eyes full of wonder. They'd left the nursery pool only a few days ago and had never seen a platypus up close.

"I'm Okipippi," she told them, her bill curling into a smile. "But everyone calls me Pippi."

"We've heard—" Tipi gushed.

"—so much—" Thuma gasped.

"—about you!" Tharta gurgled.

"Did Gee tell you I have a beak?" Pippi asked, eyeing Gee with pretend suspicion. "Because I don't! It's a bill."

"He says you're a hero," Thuma told her.

Pippi ducked her head in embarrassment. "Anyway, er, welcome to our new platypus village."

"We're very sorry—"

"—about what happened—"

"—to your old village," the triplets said.

"Me too," Pippi said with a brave smile. "But this is pretty amphibitastic."

Darel heard a doubtful note in her voice, and looked again at the half-built village. Burrows, river, trees—everything a platypus needed. Except it wasn't her real home, the place where she'd grown up. And how would *he* feel if he had to leave the Amphibilands?

Gee must have been thinking the same thing,

because he said, "We can plant bamboo along the bank, build a few bridges, and it'll be platyperfect."

Darel groaned. "That's even worse than 'amphibitastic.'"

"Poison froglings!" Pirra—Pippi's older sister—squealed from the bank. "Look! They're the coolest things ever!"

Pirra splashed into the river with a bunch of her friends and swam closer. They oohed and aahed over the brightly colored triplets, and then Pirra offered to give them a chance on the mudslide. She didn't have to ask twice. The triplets happily trailed after her.

A moment later, Pippi, Gee, and Darel were alone. "Everyone loves a poison frog," Gee said with a grin.

"Yeah," Darel said. "I wish *I* took after my dad."

"You'd look weird in yellow and purple," Gee told him.

"Not that." Darel looked toward the triplets. "I mean, if I were a Kulipari, I wouldn't be wondering what else the Rainbow Serpent wanted. I'd know *exactly* what to do: tap my poison and kick some carapace."

"You'd still look weird in yellow and purple."

"The Stargazer believed," Pippi suddenly piped up.

"Believed what?" Darel asked.

"In the Blue Sky King. She told me you were coming, back when I first met Gee. If she wasn't hibernating, she could help you figure out what the Rainbow Serpent meant."

"Can we wake her up?" Gee asked.

Pippi shook her head. "We don't even know where she is. She wanders off every few years and stays with a new tribe—like possums or lizards or emus—and sleeps for like a month."

"Emus?" Gee scoffed.

Pippi nodded. "She says it takes all kinds."

"*What* takes all kinds?" Gee asked.

"I don't know." Pippi shrugged. "'It.'"

"'All kinds.'" Darel inflated his throat thoughtfully. "Maybe it *does* take all kinds."

"And maybe you can lead a horsefly to water, but you can't make it drink," Gee told him. "Or a pinworm saved is a pinworm earned."

Pippi splashed him with her tail. "You hush!"

"What?" Gee splashed back. "I thought we were reciting dumb sayings!"

Darel plunged underwater and swam to the swirling silt of the river bottom. He hadn't seen a rainbow, and he hadn't felt the Serpent's ancient gaze upon him, but the tiny seed of an idea had taken root in his mind. The current washed over him as the seed sprouted into a vague plan. Maybe that's how the Rainbow Serpent worked. Not with a sudden shout but with hints and whispers, like ripples spreading across a quiet pond. *It takes all kinds, it takes all kinds . . .*

He kicked off the river bottom and surged upward. "The Kulipari!" he gasped when he broke the surface.

"What about them?" Gee asked.

"We're going to see them."

"Right now?"

Darel nodded, then looked to Pippi. "You've got to come, too."

"Me?" Pippi asked. "Why me?"

"Because you lived your whole life outside the Veil," Darel told her. "And you're the closest thing we have to a Stargazer."

As his crocodile surged through the water on the coast of the Amphibilands, Yabber swayed in the saddle. Lulled by the motion and the spray of seawater, he closed his eyes and sent the golden glow of his dreamcasting toward the Veil.

"This is the place," he finally murmured. "The edge of the Amphibilands."

Although the Veil covered the frog *lands* completely, it unraveled at the ocean: Neither the scorpions nor the spiders ventured into the sea. So here, where the Veil drifted apart, Yabber could send his mind inside the great dreamcasting, and learn how to reverse it.

The croc paddled water. The sun crossed the sky. Waves splashed Yabber's shell, then flowed away as he puzzled through the old king's spell.

Finally, he told his croc, "I was right. I can't do it alone. Time to go home, to the Coves."

With a happy glint in her eyes, his croc snapped at a wave, then surged forward. Yabber almost laughed at her eagerness as they passed through the Veil completely.

Then the air shimmered around them, and a nightmare vision flashed in his mind, perhaps triggered by passing through the Veil. *The frog villages lay in rubble, the streams are bone dry. The green Amphibilands are withered to a dead brown as scorpions and spiders crawl over the ruins.*

Yabber gasped in fear as the vision vanished. "Is that what happens if we *do* lower the Veil?" he muttered. "Or if we *don't* lower the Veil?"

5

PIPPI WRINKLED HER BILL AT THE SIGHT of the salt marsh, where mist drifted around gnarled trees and black water lapped at a soggy path winding between clumps of reeds. Old Jir lived in the marsh, and the Kulipari were staying with him, so Pippi took a breath and followed Darel and Gee.

She immediately regretted the breath. The marsh smelled like badly pickled fish to her. But at least she was able to keep up with the others by waddling fast on her knuckles. She'd been practicing her walking and was pretty proud of herself.

"Would you please just tell me?" Gee asked Darel again.

"Just wait!" Darel said. "We're almost there."

"Of course, your periwinkle majesty," Gee said with a deep bow. "Your wish is my command."

"Okay, okay!" Darel flared his nostrils in annoy-ance before continuing. "You know how I keep saying this whole thing with the Veil isn't only about us? Not just about the Amphibilands, I mean?"

"Sure," Gee said. "You keep saying there's something else we need to do, but you never say what you mean."

"Because I didn't know! Except 'It takes all kinds' got me thinking. How are we supposed to beat the scorps after we lower the Veil?"

"We can't," Gee told him. "That's the problem. That's why you keep croaking on about 'We need to have faith in the Serpent.' Like we're going to beat Marmoo over the head with rainbows."

Darel snorted. "We need faith *and* a plan."

"What kind of plan?"

"We need allies, Gee." Darel hopped past a clump of swamp reeds. "We need help from outside the Veil, to stand with us."

Gee looked at Pippi. "Like the platypuses."

"Exactly! Warriors from around the outback."

Pippi made a face when her knuckles sank into a swampy puddle on the path. "We're not exactly warriors."

"Entire battalions!" Darel croaked to Gee. "Entire armies. The problem is, we don't know anyone from outside."

Gee nodded slowly. "But the Kulipari do."

"And so does Pippi," Darel said with a grin.

"Oh!" Pippi swallowed. "I never really left the riverbend."

"You must know *someone*." Gee thought for a second. "How about this? Who's got the best food?"

"This is serious, Gee," Darel scolded.

"I *am* serious. Haven't you heard the saying 'An army marches on its stomach'?"

"I think that only applies to gastropods," Darel said.

Pippi was too embarrassed to ask what a gastropod was, so she just fwapped her tail against the ground. Then something splashed in the swamp nearby, and she wrinkled her bill uneasily.

"Anyway," Gee said with a snort that made Pippi think he didn't understand, either. "Who else can we ask for help?"

"There are possums," she told him as they followed the winding path past a spidery hillock of grass.

"What are they like?" Gee asked.

"Shy," she told him, "but nice."

"And they've got those cool tails, right?" Gee wiggled his butt. "Maybe they could use them as whips!"

"I kind of doubt that," Pippi told him. "Ooh,

I know! How about fish? There's carp, lungfish, perch, gudgeon—"

"*You're* a gudgeon," Gee said. "Fish can't fight scorpions."

"Oh, right." Her bill tingled, which reminded her of food. She looked into the misty swamp. "How about shrimp? I love shrimp."

"Then you're in luck," Quoba said, landing suddenly beside her.

"*Eeep!*" Pippi chirped in surprise as Gee leaped in shock and blurted, "Don't *do* that!"

"Sorry," Quoba said with a glint of humor in her eyes. "I thought you saw me there."

"You did not!" Darel laughed. "But why are we in luck?"

The tingle returned to Pippi's bill, and she smiled. "Can't you smell that?"

Darel sniffed. "Is that barbecue?"

"Yup—Ponto's special recipe," Quoba said, pointing with her staff. "Grilled shrimp in a spicy grub marinade."

Gee licked his lips. "I love shrimp!"

"I love grubs," Pippi said.

"I love grilled and spicy *and* marinade!" Gee said.

Quoba laughed and led them toward Old Jir's

house, a stump with round windows and a small twig door. They followed a stony path around back to a mossy lawn that sloped toward a forest of reeds. A flowering wonga-wonga vine climbed the wooden tables on the lawn, and Old Jir and Burnu sat at the biggest table while Ponto stood at a fire pit, wearing an apron and a chef's hat.

Instead of using tongs or a fork, he glowed briefly whenever he reached into the fire with his bare hand to turn the shrimp, using his poison to protect himself from the heat.

"Show-off," Gee called.

Ponto grinned at him and flicked a charred shrimp into the air. A tiny arrow flashed across the lawn, stabbed the shrimp, then pinned it to a plate on the biggest table.

"He's not a show-off!" Dingo announced, holding up a tiny bow with matching toothpick-arrows. "*I'm* a show-off!"

Her fingers blurred as she released a barrage of tiny arrows. The cloud of toothpicks peppered a wonga-wonga vine, then shot directly at Pippi. Before Pippi could even blink, she felt a dozen tugs at her fur. She squeezed her eyes shut . . . but didn't feel the slightest pinprick.

Then she heard the croak of Dingo's laughter. "There! Now you're dressed for a party!"

When Pippi opened her eyes, everyone was looking at her and smiling—even Old Jir—because Dingo's arrows had pinned pretty white flowers with red speckles to her fur, as if she were wearing a dozen corsages.

Her bill curled in embarrassment. "I look dumb."

"You look pretty," Darel said.

"No," Gee said. "She looks platypretty."

Pippi smiled shyly. Then everyone grabbed plates of grilled shrimp, and Ponto and Gee argued about barbecue recipes. Pippi switched to fly chips when her mouth started to burn from the spicy marinade, and she complimented Old Jir on his potato grub salad.

After a while, the conversation turned to the inevitable scorpion invasion.

"We could stomp them into jelly," Burnu said. "Except Quoba and I aren't at full power."

"You can't beat Marmoo," Old Jir said, gesturing with a toothpick. "Nobody can beat him now."

Burnu snorted. "I'd take him with one leg tied behind my back."

"Sure you would," Dingo said, tossing a shrimp into the air and catching it with her tongue. "You're the golden frog, Burnu. You're just disguised as a wart-head."

"I knew the golden frog, and even he couldn't have beaten Marmoo," Old Jir said. "Not since the spider queen wove nightcasting into Marmoo's carapace."

"Wait!" Darel's eyes bulged. "You actually *knew* the golden frog?"

"What's a golden frog?" Pippi asked.

"Ancient history," Old Jir told her with a dismissive wave of his pale hand. "Which cannot help us now. We need to focus on survival."

"We need allies." Darel set his plate aside and explained what he'd told Pippi and Gee. "And we need to bring them here before Yabber takes down the Veil."

"Except we don't know when that'll be," Dingo said.

"As soon as he can," Darel told her. "Just like the Serpent said. Yabber thinks he'll need at least a week, maybe more." He rubbed his face. "Anyway, Pippi says maybe the possums can help."

"I've been thinking," Pippi said as she toyed with a flower behind her ear. "What about the land crayfish?"

"Do you know them?" Darel asked Quoba.

She shook her head. "No, we stayed near the Coves and the swamp."

"The land crayfish . . . ," Old Jir said thoughtfully, looking to Pippi. "I haven't heard of them since before the Veil rose. You think they might help?"

She shrugged. "The Stargazer says they're nice."

"How about the paralysis ticks?" Dingo asked. "We've seen them a bunch of times."

"We've *fought* them a bunch of times," Quoba reminded her. "They're loyal to the spiders."

"Oh, right," Dingo said. "There's the burrowing cockroaches?"

"Yuck," Ponto said with a shudder. "I'm sorry, but—yuck."

"Lizards," Darel said. "They know how to fight, and Captain Killara already helped us once."

"They're mercenaries," Burnu said sourly. "I wouldn't trust them as far as you could throw Ponto."

"What about birds?" Pippi asked. "Herons or kingfishers?"

"No way," Darel said. "No birds."

"Yeah." Gee patted his gut. "This belly is irresist-ible to flying death beasts."

Pippi ducked her head. She'd forgotten that frogs were afraid of birds of prey. "Not just any birds! The Stargazer sometimes talks about the harrier hawks. And the ghost bats might still come after us. We need an ally who flies."

"She's got a point," Ponto said.

"She's also got flowers in her fur! Birds aren't going to help us. Pippi's platyposterous!" Gee paused, hoping for a laugh. "Get it? Platyposterous?"

"So that's the plan," Burnu said, ignoring Gee. "Search for allies, beg them to join us before the Veil falls, and keep our finger pads crossed that Darel's not going to get us all killed."

6

TORTOISE HEADS TURNED AS YABBER emerged from the surf and crossed the beach. Friends and neighbors nodded greetings, their eyes warm and welcoming, even if no one spoke. Yabber smiled in return. His people didn't say much—well, aside from him—but that was okay; he understood them.

Plus, the soft sand underfoot felt like home as he made his way toward the lagoon. He wanted to curl up and sleep while the sun warmed his shell, but urgency drove him onward. At least until a few hatchlings scooted around him, chanting, "Yabber's back, Yabber's back!"

"My back is what?" he asked, blinking innocently.

"Your back is *back*!" a little one said.

Yabber laughed and rapped the hatchling fondly on the shell.

When he reached the lagoon, his long-necked clan served him jellyfish on abalone shells around a driftwood fire. As the sun set, Yabber told the tale of the Snowy Mountains. He described the cave paintings showing the Hidingwar, and the one depicting the Rainbow Serpent arching over underground water holes.

He told of the fight with the spider queen and Tasmanian devils, and of melting the snow to wash them away. When he recounted his recent battle with Marmoo, mending the Veil an instant before Marmoo stung him, most of the turtles shrank slightly inside their shells.

Finally, as hatchlings snored in the shelter of their parents' flippers and moonlight glinted over the waves, Yabber said, "And now the Amphibilands prepares again for war."

"So you will strengthen the Veil," an old turtle said, nodding.

"King Sergu raised the Veil to save the Amphibilands," Yabber told her. "But he never wanted it to stand forever. He never wanted the frogs to live apart from the rest of the outback. He once asked, 'Does the Veil keep the scorpions out, or the frogs in?'"

The old turtle thought about that. And thought about it, and thought about it . . .

"He was convinced," Yabber continued, when he

realized the old turtle wasn't going to say anything, "that one day the scorpions and frogs and spiders would live together in harmony. In fact, he'd hoped that Queen Jarrah would lead her people to join us in peace. That's why he taught her to dreamcast."

"But she betrayed him," a sea turtle said.

Yabber nodded. "But now there's been a vision."

"Of what?" a turtle mother asked, rubbing the belly of a hatchling sleeping on his back beside her. "What did you see?"

"I saw the Rainbow Serpent," Yabber said. "But someone else talked to it."

Murmurs of wonder sounded around the fire. The turtles honored the Rainbow Serpent, the ancient spirit who spread life across the outback, but they hadn't spoken with it since the days of legend, when the Serpent taught them dreamcasting.

"Who?" the old turtle asked. "The platypus Stargazer?"

"Darel," Yabber announced.

A voice in the darkness said, "Who?"

"Darel the wood frog."

"Never heard of him."

Yabber curved his neck peevishly. "The one who hopped all this way to ask for King Sergu's help!"

"Oh!" the voice said. "You mean the chubby one."

Yabber sighed. "That's Gee."

"Right. The wood frog."

"That's not important." Yabber looked at the flickering flames. "What's important is that the Rainbow Serpent told him to take down the Veil."

A stunned silence fell, and the first rays of sunrise crept over the horizon before someone said, "How will the frogs survive?"

"I don't know," Yabber admitted.

"Does this Darel know what he's doing?"

"I, uh . . ." Yabber swallowed. "Yes. Yes, I think he does."

"So what will you do?"

"Take down the Veil," Yabber said. "But I need your help."

7

A BUTCHER-BIRD CRIED AS THE SCORpions marched through the swamp toward the spiders' mountain.

"The spiders tore the Veil once," Lord Marmoo muttered. "They can do it again."

Pigo didn't respond. He just stayed in position, his tail held high, as night creatures hooted in the gloom and tree branches cast shadows like skeleton arms.

"The spiders tore the Veil once," Lord Marmoo murmured an hour later as he stepped from the swamp. "They can do it again."

Pigo still didn't respond. He simply led the squad of red-banded soldiers uphill, keeping them in a disciplined row. Lord Marmoo had repeated the same phrase all day and Pigo had stopped replying an hour ago, telling himself that his lord was merely determined, not losing his mind.

When they reached the mines, a squad of spider

archers swung down from the trees. "L–L–Lord Marmoo?" the one in front asked.

"The spiders tore the Veil once," Marmoo told the spider, his main eyes dark with purpose. "They can do it again."

The spider bowed nervously. "Are . . . are you here to see the new queen being crowned, my lord?"

Lord Marmoo stung the spider, and flung the body aside. "The spiders tore the Veil once," he announced. "You will do it again."

The other spiders didn't raise their bows or uncoil their silk. They simply stared at Lord Marmoo in frozen terror as he marched past.

On the mountaintop, the spider queen's castle rose like an immense pile of boulders. Black webs draped the rocky spires, to honor Queen Jarrah's death, and dark cobwebs shrouded the front doors. Pigo cleared a path across the silken moat for his lordship, then skittered into the great hall—and scowled.

A mesh of cobwebs filled the huge chamber, like the thick foliage of the Amphibilands or a supernaturally dense fog.

"*Spiders,*" Pigo groused, as he hacked a path through the cobwebs.

He headed for the stairway that rose to the rooftop

throne room, swiping and snipping with his pincers. Lord Marmoo trailed behind Pigo, making no sound except for the clicking of his feet on the floor. The silence worried Pigo, but he focused on his task, clearing a trail until he reached the rooftop.

Then he glanced at his lordship—and swallowed a cry of shock.

Lord Marmoo was covered with elaborate swirls and dotted lines, eerie patterns etched into his carapace where the feathery cobwebs had touched him.

Pigo felt his mid-legs buckle slightly. "My lord? The webs . . . Should I brush them away?"

"Leave them," Lord Marmoo told him. "They'll show these crawlers what I really am."

What are you? Pigo wondered.

"Born with a scorpion's strength," Marmoo continued, "and reborn through a spider's magic."

They strode past parapets and terraces as they approached the throne. Pigo tensed at the sight of spiders massed around a high polished platform. Moments ago, they must have been watching the throne on top of the platform, but now all the spider warriors were staring at Lord Marmoo.

Lord Marmoo didn't seem to notice. He kept walking, and the spiders parted for him.

Seated on the throne was a spider Pigo recognized. She'd been one of Queen Jarrah's ladies-in-waiting, and he'd spoken to her while they had waited for Jarrah to return from the Snowy Mountains. She'd been a good source of information at the time, but she looked more aloof now, as her own lady-in-waiting stood beside her, holding a silver crown.

"Welcome, Lord Marmoo," she said in a chilly voice. "I am Lady Fahlga, soon to be *Queen* Fahlga."

The patterns along Marmoo's carapace gleamed. "The spider queen tore the Veil once. You will do it again."

A hint of uncertainty crossed Fahlga's face. "I am not—*yet*—as powerful as Jarrah was."

"The spiders tore the Veil once," Lord Marmoo repeated. "You will do it again."

"I'm not sure if I can."

"Then you're not fit to rule," Lord Marmoo said, batting away spiders as he strode toward the throne.

"Stop him!" Fahlga cried. "Stop him!"

Webbing flashed at Marmoo—but when it touched his web-etched carapace, it dissolved into dust. The spiders hissed and scuttled in dismay, and Lord Marmoo leaped atop the high polished platform and snatched the crown from the lady-in-waiting.

"The day of the spider is done!" he declared. "You are now part of the scorpion kingdom!"

"Not so long as I am queen," Fahlga snarled.

"You aren't." Lord Marmoo raised the crown above his own head. "And never will be."

A shock ran through the spider ranks—and through Pigo's heart as well—when Marmoo lowered the crown onto his own head. "M-m-my lord," he stuttered. "Is it right for one species to rule another?"

Lord Marmoo tilted his head as he examined Pigo. "Beware, little brother, that you don't grow soft and weak."

Fear tightened Pigo's stomach. "Yes, my lord."

"Well, my lady?" Lord Marmoo asked Fahlga. "Will you bow to your new king?"

She stood from her throne, quietly defiant, though Pigo thought he saw fear in her eyes.

"Commander Pigo," Marmoo said, "sting her."

Pigo whipped his tail toward the spider lady's thorax—then stopped, an inch away.

"Are you disobeying me?" Lord Marmoo snarled to Pigo. "Explain yourself!"

"M-m-my lord," Pigo said. "Lady Fahlga helped

us when you were at the mercy of the queen's magic."

"But now the queen is dead. Sting her!"

"As you command, my lord," Pigo said, drawing back his tail for the killing blow.

"I have information!" Fahlga blurted. "Information you need."

"Tell me," Lord Marmoo demanded.

"The frogs trekked high into the Snowy Mountains—"

Lord Marmoo scoffed. "That's old news."

"But this isn't," Fahlga said, straightening slightly. "They met the Rainbow Serpent on the mountaintop. And I know what the Serpent told the wood frog named Darel."

There was a sudden chill in the air, and Pigo cringed. Lord Marmoo hated the Rainbow Serpent and the young frog with a blind rage, and sometimes he rampaged at the mere mention of their names. But this time, Marmoo simply hunched inside his carapace and glowered.

"The Serpent wants the frogs to lower the Veil," the spider lady said.

Suspicion flickered in Marmoo's ruined face. "No. You lie."

"I vow that this is true."

"Is that so?" Marmoo snorted. "Did the frogs tell you?"

"I'm not Queen Jarrah," the lady told him. "I don't rule as she did. I keep in touch with the spider tribes scattered across the outback. A tiny spider in a hidden web can overhear a great many things—and, eventually, the news comes to me."

"And from this point forth," Marmoo said, "everything you learn, you will share with me."

"I will," she said, bowing her head. "My king."

"They are going to lower the Veil themselves?" Marmoo's side eyes narrowed. "Even frogs are not that stupid."

"They are. You have my word as a nightcaster . . . and a loyal subject."

Lord Marmoo stared at her for a few seconds. Then his triumphant laugh echoed across the rooftop, and he lowered Pigo's tail with one of his pincers.

"They're serving themselves to me on a platter!" he crowed. "Without the Veil, they're not an army of frogs—they're a meal."

8

THE VILLAGE WAS QUIET, ALMOST AS IF it were holding its breath. Darel hadn't expected a parade, but the stillness made him a little nervous.

"Are you sure about this?" he asked Gee as they walked toward the billabong to meet Ponto.

"You mean about searching the outback for anyone dumb enough to help us when we let the scorpions invade?" Gee asked. "Not totally."

"Well, when you put it *that* way, it doesn't sound so good."

Gee grinned. "How about, uh, 'Seeking brave warriors to help us follow the Rainbow Serpent's plan'?"

"That's way better," Darel said with a snort. "But I meant, are you sure you want to come?"

"I have to. Last time you went off alone, you almost got eaten by a Tasmanian devil."

"Good luck, boys," a burrowing frog called from his hole. "Stay safe."

Other burrowing frogs croaked, "Good-bye," and "Try not to get killed," and "I hope you know what you're doing." Farther along, a crowd of somber wood frogs wished them well. Then one said, "We're trusting you, Darel. Don't let us down."

"I won't," Darel said, and barely kept himself from adding *I hope*.

When he and Gee reached the billabong, Arabanoo was sitting on a low branch, watching Coorah mess with her backpack below him.

"What're you doing?" Darel asked her, hopping closer.

"Organizing my supplies. Bandages here, pastes here, splints here. Ointments, powders—" She slung the pack onto her back and stood. "I'm coming."

"Your dad said it's okay?"

"Of course. Traveling with you two is the best way to learn to heal bleeding gashes and broken bones."

"'Bleeding gashes and broken bones,'" Gee repeated with a moan.

"Plus," Coorah said brightly, "there are wasps out there that sting eggs into your brain! I'd love to learn how to dig those out."

"Suddenly I don't feel so good," Gee muttered.

"Actually, Dad wouldn't let me come until Old Jir talked to him," Coorah admitted.

"Old Jir said he needs me in the village," Arabanoo told them. "Working on the defenses."

"Standing guard is noble work!" Dingo strolled toward the billabong. "You and me, tree frog."

The earth shook when Ponto landed beside Coorah. His spiked bracers looked freshly sharpened, and his pouch of herbs was almost as full as Coorah's.

"Everyone ready?" he asked in his deep rumble.

"I am," Coorah said, taking a breath.

Darel nodded. "Let's do this."

"What if the Veil falls before you get back?" Arabanoo asked. "Before you get help? Yabber says he's not sure exactly what'll happen when he starts lowering it."

Anxiety coiled in Darel's stomach. "I barely slept last night, worrying about that. We'll just have to do this as quickly as possible. The truth is, by lowering the Veil, we're already putting ourselves completely in the Serpent's hands."

"That's a great idea," Dingo said. "Considering serpents don't even have hands."

"We just need to do our best," Darel continued,

ignoring her, "to find allies before Marmoo attacks. The Rainbow Serpent told us to lower the Veil, so that's what we'll do."

For a moment, nobody spoke, like his answer wasn't good enough. He kind of agreed, but he didn't know what else to say. He groped in his mind for inspiration, but all he found was his mother croaking, "Trust and faith."

"So *now* is everyone ready?" Ponto asked into the silence.

"I'm ready for anything," Gee said. "Except brain-stinging wasps."

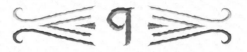

ON THE FAR SIDE OF THE BILLABONG, the path narrowed into faint trails that branched through the dense underbrush. Then even those trails disappeared, and the untamed hills rose toward the Veil and the distant mountains beyond.

Ponto trampled a path through thornbushes and briar patches. He didn't seem to notice the thistles or spikes, but Darel, Coorah, and Gee kept flinching as they pricked their toes. Finally, Coorah hopped a few steps on one foot, then sat and dug in her pack for strips of thick cloth.

"Wrap your feet," she told Darel and Gee, tossing them strips.

"My toes still ache from when Darel and I crossed the desert," Gee told her, weaving a strip through his toe pads.

"What're you doing?" Ponto called from uphill. "Silly wood frogs!"

"We don't all have scaly reptile toes like you," Darel told him, wrapping his toes.

Ponto lifted one foot. "That's one hundred per-cent frogskin, tadpole."

Twenty minutes later, with a swath of flattened undergrowth behind them, they reached the Veil. The landscape changed from a lush, prickly green to a drab olive, and Darel frowned thoughtfully, feeling like he should say a few words. Maybe something about hope and loyalty, and how if everyone joins together—

"Let's move," Gee said, leaping ahead.

Ponto sprang after him. "Look before you leap, frogling!"

"C'mon, D," Coorah called.

An itchy tingle spread across Darel's skin when he leaped through the Veil. On the other side, the air smelled harsh and abrasive, and the dense under-brush turned into scattered trees hunched over crusty vines and parched weeds.

Coorah smacked her lips. "My tongue feels like I swallowed a puffball."

"We're only a day from the possums," Ponto said, shading his eyes to scan the foothills.

Gee frowned. "We should've taken a shortcut through the platypus village."

"Marmoo might be watching," Ponto told him.

"Then you could stomp him with your lizard feet!"

Ponto shook his head. "He'd cut me down in a second, Gee. Until we know how to beat him, we've got to stay away." He pointed farther into the hills. "There. Over that hill with the koala ears."

As they hopped through the scrubby foothills, the words *Until we know how to beat him* echoed in Darel's mind. The problem was, they didn't know how. Maybe the shy possums also hunted scorpions. Sure, or maybe the crayfish—

A squeal shattered the quiet afternoon. Darel drew his dagger and spun toward the sound. It was Coorah, staring at a vine with long leaves and wilted yellow flowers.

Darel scanned for threats. Hunting birds? Thorny lizards? Scorpions or spiders or—

"It's a snake"—Coorah squealed—"vine!"

"A *what*?" Darel asked, jumping closer.

"Snake vine!" she announced, pointing at the ground. "Can you smell that?"

Darel wrinkled his nose. "Disgusting."

"That's snake vine," she told him. "It doesn't grow in the Amphibilands, but it's great for rashes."

"You squealed because you saw a *plant*?"

"I didn't squeal," she said. "I exclaimed."

Darel sheathed his dagger in disgust. "Would you tell her?" he asked Ponto.

"Sure." Ponto stepped beside Coorah and examined the vine. "Good eyes, Coorah. I missed that."

"That's not what you're supposed to tell her!" Darel said.

"Oh," Ponto said, and tried again. "Well, snake vine's not just for rashes. You can also use it to treat sores. You crush the leaves to a powder and mix it with—"

"Not that, either!" Darel interrupted. "Tell her she shouldn't scream. She almost gave me a heart attack."

"Look on the bright side," Gee told him. "If you did have a heart attack, they could probably cure you with the snake vine."

"Everyone's a joker," Darel said.

By the time they had reached the koala-eared hill, the sun was slipping behind the mountains. They pitched tents in the shade of Wollemi pines, ate a quick dinner, then headed to the top of one of the rocky "ears," which made a good lookout point.

"According to the platypuses," Coorah said, pointing into the distance, "the possum village is over that pointy hill, beyond a ravine."

Darel looked toward the hill. "No smoke. Maybe Marmoo hasn't found and destroyed it yet."

"Or maybe he's setting a trap," Ponto said.

IRY SHRUBS WERE SCATTERED across the red-brown earth of the outback. Pigo took a deep breath of sandblasted air, and his mouthparts almost formed a smile. It smelled like home.

The spider servants carrying Lady Fahlga in her silken litter didn't seem to appreciate it, though. They hunched and hissed and peered into the empty expanse with suspicious eyes.

When Pigo finally led them into the scorpion encampment, they scuttled quickly to the silken building that Queen Jarrah had woven. Once inside, they seemed to relax, and Fahlga and her ladies crawled from the litter.

She sent her servants off to weave shelters for her soldiers, then shaped a simple triangular web in the center of the room. When she bared her fangs, drops of poison splashed onto the webbing. Then she nodded, and her ladies-in-waiting started circling the triangle.

As Pigo watched, the spiders added layer after layer of silk, expanding the web into a funnel, which grew until it was almost as big as he was.

A moment after Fahlga and her ladies stopped circling their webbed creation, Lord Marmoo shoved aside the front flap. "Are your spiders ready for war?" he grunted.

"The legions are following close behind," Fahlga told him. "My generals are—"

"*My* generals."

Lady Fahlga bowed her head. "*Your* generals are assembling every archer, as you commanded. My—*your*—servants are weaving them tents as we speak. They'll arrive before nightfall."

"And the rest?" Lord Marmoo asked. "The ghost bats, the blue-banded bees, every creature Jarrah ever commanded?"

Fahlga stroked the funnel web. "This will bring them to you."

"When?"

"Now," she said, and her eyes turned black.

The next morning, a harsh grinding noise awoke Darel. His heart jerked in his chest and he rolled into a crouch, ready to fight—until he realized that the sound was Coorah crushing snake vine into powder with a stone.

"Whoa," she said. "You're a little edgy."

"Yeah, I wonder why." Darel pretended to think about it. "Maybe because we're lowering the Veil to let the scorpions destroy our home."

"Or maybe because you're grumpy every morning," she said.

After breakfast, they broke camp. The sun rose higher and the day turned hotter—and eventually scorching—as they hopped closer to the pointy hill. Even the cloth strips around his feet didn't keep Darel's toe pads from burning, and his skin throbbed with thirst. The hours passed in an aching blur of spiky undergrowth and sharp-edged rocks.

Finally, they reached the edge of a deep canyon with jagged sides for easy climbing.

"We cross this ravine," Ponto said when Darel and the others caught up with him. "Climb the hill, and we're in possum territory."

"You're forgetting the first step," Gee said. "Snack time!"

He headed for a shrub with heart-shaped leaves, pulling his pack from his shoulder—and Ponto tackled him.

"Hey!" Gee yelped. "There's enough for everyone."

"That's a gympie-gympie," Ponto said, nodding toward the shrub. "The most poisonous of the outback's trees."

Coorah looked at the bush. "*That* little thing?"

"It's covered with toxic stinging hairs, each one like a wasp's sting—except the pain lasts for weeks."

"On second thought," Gee said, looking in the other direction. "Let's have snack time over *there*."

"We'll reach the possums today." Coorah plopped down and dangled her legs over the edge of the ravine. "How long to the crayfish?"

Ponto shrugged. "I thought we'd reach the possums this morning. You wood frogs hop slower than a one-legged cricket."

"You're just jealous, because we're—" Darel spotted a white cloud unraveling over the hills. "Hmm . . . weird."

"Speak for yourself," Coorah said. "I'm not weird."

"Not us." Darel pointed. "*That*. What is it?"

"Ghost bats," Gee said, his voice tight. "I thought we beat the last of them at the platypus village."

"There's dozens of bat colonies around." Ponto cracked his knuckles. "Which is good—I need the exercise."

"C'mon!" Darel hopped to his feet. "We can't fight them."

"Speak for yourself," Ponto told him.

Darel slitted his nostrils with annoyance. "What if they spot us? They'll tell Marmoo that we're heading for the possum village."

"Oh," Ponto said. "Good point."

"Everyone get out of sight!" Darel urged. "Hide in the ravine!"

"Hiding's my specialty," Gee said, leaping past Darel into the ravine.

"Go, go, go!" Darel croaked at Ponto.

Ponto was big, but when he moved, he *moved*. A yellow streak flashed past Darel and disappeared into the ravine. As the swarm of ghost bats swirled closer, Coorah vaulted over a clump of grass and fell from sight—and an eyeblink later, Darel followed.

He landed on an outcropping, then hopped lower to the trunk of a cliffside shrub. He dropped to a ledge, then rebounded from the steep wall to another outcropping far below. The walls of the ravine loomed above him, casting the world in shadow, and cool air touched his skin. He landed on the floor of the ravine beside a boulder, where Ponto was hunched, his bright yellow looking duller in the shade.

Small, polished pebbles shifted and clacked under Darel's toe pads. "They're like river rocks," he said, grabbing a handful and letting them tumble through his fingers.

"This must've been a stream once," Ponto said, his normally booming voice soft.

"Out here?" Coorah said. "It's too dry."

"The turtle king said that water used to flow freely across the outback," Ponto explained.

Darel nodded, thinking about that—and about the turtle king. "I wonder what he'd say about all this."

"About lowering the Veil?" Coorah asked.

"Yeah."

"Knowing that old shell-head," Ponto said with a fond smile, "I bet he saw all this coming. I bet that's exactly why he picked you to lead us."

"Because nobody else is dumb enough to—" Darel stopped suddenly. "Where's Gee?"

"Gee?" Coorah called softly. "Gee!"

There was no answer. No sign of Gee.

11

IPPI DOVE INTO THE RIVER SHALLOWS, closed her eyes, and wriggled her bill in the silt. Muddy water billowed around her as she swiveled her head, but she didn't feel any tingling. She opened her eyes, swam to the surface, took a breath, and dove again.

This time, she felt the tingle in her bill that meant there was food nearby—a bunch of water bug larvae. She gobbled them down, then swam to the surface and smacked her tail happily at the midmorning snack.

She noticed a bunch of platypuses on the shoreline looking at her, but she pretended not to see them. She didn't mind that everyone treated her like an ambassador to the frog village, carrying messages back and forth. But sometimes the other platypuses acted like she was the Stargazer, which made her nervous.

She didn't know how to read the Rainbow Serpent's messages in trickles of water. She didn't know any of the answers. All she knew was that the platypuses had to fight alongside the frogs to protect their new home—the Amphibilands. And nobody wanted to hear that.

She dove again, gobbled a few more larvae, then peeked back toward the shoreline.

Nobody was looking at her anymore. Instead, they were gazing toward an oak tree, where four white-lipped tree frogs crouched on a branch. She swam closer just as Arabanoo hopped down to stand in front of the platypuses.

"—and Coorah and Gee are crossing the outback right now," he was saying. "They're asking other tribes to fight for the Amphibilands and the Rainbow Serpent. And I'm here to ask the same of you."

The crowd of platypuses shifted and murmured, and an older platypus said, "We're not warriors."

"Neither are we," Arabanoo said. "But we'll fight to defend our home and families. Just like you fought the ghost bats."

Another murmur ran through the platypuses, and Pippi caught a few words: *That's true*, and *We beat them, too*, and *Frogs helped us when we needed . . .*

"But you're asking us to stand against the scorpion lord," the older platypus said. "We'll die if we fight him. All of us, from the oldest gray-fur to the youngest platypup. And so will you. We saw Marmoo destroy our riverbend village. He's not natural. He's not normal. How are we supposed to fight *that*?"

Arabanoo's shoulders slumped. "I don't know."

A blur of color landed on the shoreline beside Arabanoo, and the platypups gasped. Burnu scanned the crowd, then caught one of his boomerangs, which had twirled at him from behind the oak.

"We don't have a single chance," he announced. "If we don't fight."

"And if we do?" Pippi's mother asked.

For once, Burnu's cockiness faded. "I don't know," he said softly. "I don't know if we can win."

"We can't fight on dry land," the older platypus said. "We can barely *walk* on dry land. I'm sorry—we can't help you."

"We can't fight on dry land," Pippi called, swimming closer. "But in the water, no scorp can touch us. We can hold the rivers and the ponds."

"Pippi . . . ," her mother said gently. "We're not warriors."

"That doesn't mean we're not *fighters*," she said.

"What can we do?" her sister asked.

"We can carry messages and bring supplies," Pippi said. "And if we have to, we can fight. The scorps will laugh when they see us—just like everyone does." She stepped onto the riverbank. "Then they'll feel our spurs."

The cooler air of the ravine whooshed past as Gee landed on a rocky slope and jumped around a curve, out of sight of the ghost bats. He grinned to himself and dropped into a wide, jagged crevice below him.

He was completely invisible from above.

He grunted in satisfaction, and followed the crevice to the ravine floor. No bats in sight. No frogs in sight, either, so he hopped across a clearing of hard-packed earth, heading toward Darel and the others.

Once he crossed the clearing, something tugged at his ankle—probably Darel, pulling him to safety.

"Hey!" he croaked, jerking his leg. "You can let go! The bats can't see me!"

The grip didn't loosen, and when Gee turned to look, his eyes bulged in shock.

The clearing of hard-packed earth wasn't there anymore. Instead, a dark mouth opened in the ground, and a sticky rope lashed around his ankle like a thick, pale tongue. Gee took a breath to shout for help but—*swoosh!*—the rope dragged him into the pitch-black mouth.

Except it wasn't a mouth. It was an underground cave—and the "clearing of hard-packed earth" slammed shut overhead. Like a trapdoor.

Gee fell through darkness, hit a sloped surface, and rolled. He grabbed the floor with his toe pads, screamed "Help!" and launched himself at the roof in a panic. Halfway there, the sticky rope around his ankle tightened. He jerked to a halt midair, then crashed back down.

He whimpered in fear. Then his heart clenched as the rope dragged him deeper into the darkness.

"Stop!" he shrieked, his eyes bulging in terror. "No! Show yourself, you wart-headed worm! I am Gurnugan Bat-foe! I'll—*Gurk!*" He slid into a sticky mess of . . . ugh, something sticky and messy . . . and he heard the faint chittering of mandibles in the darkness.

"I'm a close personal friend of the Blue Sky King!" he shouted, his voice shaking.

As his eyes adjusted to the dark, he saw that a steep earthen ramp rose above him in a large cavern with pebble-mosaic floors and walls. He gulped when he noticed that the designs looked like spiders, all jagged and predatory. The cavern disappeared into the darkness around him, and a half-dozen other ramps angled upward toward the ceiling—probably toward more trapdoors.

"It had to happen one day," he said. "Someone was bound to realize that I'm the tastiest treat alive."

He tugged at the rope around his ankle and realized that it was a strand of spider silk. He groaned softly. *Spiders*. A nest of underground spiders.

And that's when he saw a big dark shape descending toward him from the ceiling. Eight legs.

Huge abdomen. Way too many eyes. And fangs. Big, gleaming fangs spread wide.

Gee whimpered as the spider spun lower, until her furry forelegs quivered inches from his face, and her fangs spread wider.

"Oh, ribbit," Gee said under his breath.

"A frog?" the spider asked. "Are you a frog?"

"I'm a Curdle Frog!" Gee blurted. "Sour as a pickled lemon!"

"Sour?" the spider said, a few of her eyes twinkling in the gloom. "I love sour."

"—is what you'd *think* I'd taste like," Gee said, scrambling frantically. "But actually I taste like feet. Like sweaty, hairy, mammal feet."

The spider's fangs spread even wider—in what Gee suddenly realized was a smile. Then she chittered and announced, "I like frogs! You're funny."

"We are! I am! Frog—funny!"

"I thought you were a lizard."

"Do I *look* scaly?"

She chittered again. "They've been slinking around, trying to find a way in for the scorpion lord. But a frog?" She slashed at him with her fangs, cutting through the silk binding his ankle. "I never met a hopper before."

Gee cautiously wiped the remaining web from his leg. "Then this is your lucky day. I'm Gee."

"No way!" she said, rearing back. "You're *Gee*!"

He puffed out his throat proudly. "You've heard of me? I didn't think the tales of my daring adventures had traveled quite so far."

"What? No. I'm Effie. We're Eff and Gee." She waved a few forelegs. "Isn't that neat?"

"Not as neat as the tales of my daring adventures."

"C'mon! I'll show you around!"

She scuttled into the darkness, and Gee eyed the trapdoor overhead, ready to make a break for it. He crouched, tensing his legs to leap upward.

"Are you hungry?" Effie's voice echoed in the cave. "I've got a whole ceiling full of honeypot ants!"

Gee untensed his legs. It was hard to find food in the outback, so maybe he could resupply with honeypot ants. Though he really should tell Darel and the others where he was, or they'd worry and—

A strand of silk shot from the gloom and Effie yanked him toward her. "C'mon!" she said with a chitter as he staggered beside her. "Let's go!"

He pulled the webbing off himself. "Would you stop that?"

"Sorry," Effie said, ducking her head as she led him

toward a side cave. "I've just never showed anyone around before. Where are you from?"

"The Amphibilands."

She gasped—and so did the four or five other spiders hidden in the darkness around them. "That's a real place?"

"The realest. So! This is your home, huh?"

"Pretty cool, right?" she said. "Never gets hot, even if it's a scorcher aboveground."

Farther inside the cave, a row of torches flickered with bright, smokeless flames, and Gee got his first clear view of the mosaics. Colorful, polished river rocks swirled in patterns from floor to ceiling, depicting spiders in branching tunnels that spread through the earth. In one corner, a rainbow arced down, through a mosaic trapdoor, then swirled along the tunnels and into what looked like a vast underground river.

"Whoa!" Gee said. "Is that water?"

"'Course it is," Effie said.

He scratched his forehead, dubious. "Underground?"

"That's where water comes from, silly!" She chittered again. "I'll show you! C'mon."

12

YABBER AND THE THREE APPRENTICE dreamcasters swam toward the Amphibilands. A forest of bright coral blurred past beneath them, and Yabber wondered—not for the first time—if the beauty of the reef was related to that of the Rainbow Serpent.

"We're almost at the Veil," he said, his excitement growing as he paddled steadily. "And then you're in for a treat that will completely blow your shells. You think the mangrove swamp is something? Well, the Amphibilands is something *else*. The frogs built one of the marvels of the outback, with leaf villages and burrows and tree houses and—well! The creeks and ponds overflow with happy croaking."

"Not for long," one of the apprentices said. "Not after we let the scorpions in. Then there will be pain and horror and death the likes of which the outback has never seen."

Yabber opened his mouth . . . but didn't say

anything. Once they arrived in the Amphibilands, they'd start unraveling the Veil. Allowing Marmoo's troops to rampage across every village, every burrow, every stream and pond.

Gee followed Effie deeper into the spider cavern, hopping low so he didn't hit his head on the ceiling.

She stopped suddenly in a round chamber and gestured toward a dark shape in the gloom. "Oh, that's my sister. Say hi!"

"Hi!" Gee said.

"Not you!" Effie chittered at him. "I meant her."

"Hello," her sister whispered, then crawled away.

Effie showed Gee her fangy smile. "She's shy. Oh! And that's my other sister, and my *other* other sister . . . and my web is down that tunnel. I collect nuts."

Gee grinned. "You *are* nuts."

"Silly!" Effie whacked him with a furry foreleg, then scampered along the wall and through a dark cave mouth.

Gee felt a brush of moist air on his skin. "Was that a rainbow in the mosaic?"

"The Serpent," Effie said, a few of her eyes fixed on him. "Don't you know about the Rainbow Serpent?"

"Of course I do! I didn't know *you* did!"

"Are you kidding? We're its spideriest fans!" Effie said as she led him around a curve into a massive tunnel. "The Serpent's the one who told us to dig deeper like this, and not just build trapdoors."

"It told the platypuses the same thing—to dig deeper," Gee said thoughtfully.

"Platypuses aren't real!" Effie laughed, then gestured with a foreleg. "Here we are!"

The moistness in the air tasted good through Gee's skin as he stared into the torchlit distance. He and Effie were standing on the shore of an under-ground river. Or what was left of one. Only a trickle of water remained, and a handful of spiders were filling web-baskets with water and hauling them away.

Gee looked downstream, where the trickle disap-peared into the darkness. "How far does it go?"

"Nobody knows," Effie told him. "The diggers kept going until they met another bunch of tunnels, then turned back."

"All for that tiny little stream?"

"It used to be bigger. There used to be ten times as much water."

"I've got an important question," Gee said, his throat bulging.

Effie nodded seriously. "What's that?"

"Can I jump in?"

She chittered and shoved him with a foreleg toward the water. Gee contentedly settled himself in the middle of the little stream, watching Effie climb the wall and pluck ripe round berries from the ceiling. When she tossed them to him, he flicked his tongue and realized they weren't berries—they were honeypot ants. *Delicious.* He rolled onto his back in the trickle. The water tasted rocky, but fresh, and he wondered where it came from. And also why the Rainbow Serpent had told the spiders to dig tunnels. Well, maybe Darel would—

"Oh, no!" Gee blurted, sitting up.

"What's wrong?" Effie said, lowering herself beside him on a thread of webbing.

"My friends!" He hopped toward the exit. "I've got to tell them I'm okay."

"That's not the fastest way," Effie said, unspooling silk at him. "Hold on tight!"

He grabbed the silk, then spun slowly in the air as Effie climbed upward. She pulled him higher and higher through the cave. The riverbed disappeared beneath him, and he rose into a vertical earthen shaft that ran straight up and down.

A half-dozen spiders greeted Effie, then gaped at

Gee and whispered things like "Poor dear, it's only got four legs."

A minute later, Effie pulled Gee into the first cavern—the one with the ramps—and pointed to a trapdoor. "That's the one you came through, so—"

A crash echoed in the cavern. One of the trapdoors was ripped from the ceiling, and light flooded into the gloom. Gee raised his hand to shield his eyes from the brightness.

Ponto's voice boomed out. "Spiders! Release our friend or suffer the consequences."

Gee lowered his hand and saw Ponto, Darel, and Coorah in a beam of bright sunlight. Ponto's colors looked intensely vivid, though he hadn't tapped his poison—and even Darel and Coorah almost seemed to glow.

"I'm okay!" Gee said, hopping forward. "Sorry! I'm okay!"

"Gee!" Darel dropped through the trapdoor into the cavern. "Thank frog you're all right."

"If these spiders touched a wart on your head," Ponto said, falling to the floor, then glowering around him.

"They're nice!" Gee said. He beckoned Effie to come closer. "This is Effie. My friend."

Effie crept toward the light. For a second, she looked scared. Then she chittered, "I hope one of you is named Aitch, and another is Eye!"

Gee croaked a laugh. "Ha!"

"I don't get it," Coorah said, wrinkling her fore-head.

"All you've got to get," Gee told her, "is that not all spiders are bad."

"Are you sure?" Darel asked, glancing suspiciously into the mosaic cavern.

"Of course I'm sure! Just look at her! Plus, she gave me water."

"*Friendly* spiders?" Darel smiled at Effie. "Well, you learn something new every day."

"So you didn't even get bitten, even a *little*?" Coorah asked Gee with a sigh. "I mean, I wouldn't mind learning how to heal a spider bite."

"Maybe later," Gee told her, then introduced everyone.

Effie brought water and honeypot ants and called the "spider mothers"—who were like the chiefs. They sat in a circle around the lighted section of the cavern and listened as Darel told them the story of the Amphibilands. He explained about Lord Marmoo and Queen Jarrah—and about old King Sergu and the quest to the Snowy Mountains to meet the Rainbow Serpent.

". . . and now the Rainbow Serpent wants us to tear down the Veil, our only defense against Marmoo." Darel turned from one spider mother to the next. "We need friends to stand with us. We need you."

13

N ARCH OF ROCKS ROSE FROM THE
sand, looking like the spine of some
immense, long-dead beast. Pigo and
Lady Fahlga followed Lord Marmoo
from the lowest rock toward the high-
est one, then paused a step below him.

A sea of scorpions covered the sands in front
of Pigo, tails held high, stingers swaying. Flanking
them were spider battalions, hunched beneath silken
awnings. A few taipan snakes dozed atop a flat rock,
and lizard mercenaries hunkered behind them—all
except Captain Killara's troop, which Lord Marmoo
planned to hunt down after he finished with the
Amphibilands for having betrayed him in the battle
against the frogs.

A flock of ghost bats clung to the shady underside
of the arching rocks, white wings wrapped around their
bodies, ears swiveling to track the swarms of blue-
banded bees buzzing beneath them. Lord Marmoo
had ordered them not to feed, though. At least, not yet.

His lordship raised one pincer, and silence fell.

"Water is life!" Lord Marmoo shouted, his voice rasping across the dunes. "Even for those of us born to the desert. And yet the frogs hoard water. They lock it away in their lakes and ponds, while all of you go thirsty."

An angry murmuring spread among the spider troops.

"But very soon now," Lord Marmoo said, "the Veil will fall. Not just tear, not just rip. It will *vanish*, and we will march!"

Raucous cheers erupted from the troops, and Lord Marmoo lifted a pincer triumphantly. Then he murmured under his breath, "And during the next few days, Pigo, you and I shall lead a squad on a mission."

"What sort of mission, my lord?" Pigo asked, equally quiet.

"The frogs are soft and weak," Lord Marmoo said, "but they're sly. I won't underestimate them again. We'll prepare a little surprise . . ."

Darel headed away from the ravine, his stomach bulging with spider water and his mind swimming with worries.

Beside him, Gee toyed with the web-bracelet Effie had given him. "Who knew spiders could be so great?"

"If they were so great," Darel grumped, "they would've agreed to help us."

"They *can't* help," Gee told him. "They're afraid to leave the cavern. Effie told me there used to be ten times as many of them before the underground river dried up. You can't blame them for being afraid."

"They *did* give me silkweb bandages!" Coorah said, patting her bag of supplies. "Which was nice. Except . . ." Her voice turned troubled. "I don't want anyone to get hurt. Not anymore."

"Yeah," Gee said. "It's not practice now."

Coorah frowned. "It's real. Too real."

Darel barely heard them. He was too busy kicking himself for his failure with the trapdoor spiders. He should've said something different, something better. He should have convinced them. He should've made them believe. But how? How do you ask someone to take a wild leap of faith?

And what about those tunnels under the spider cavern, and that trickle of water? Was that part of the Rainbow Serpent's plan?

Well, maybe he'd do better with the possums.

He sighed, and followed Ponto across the outback.

Hours passed. The sun lowered in the sky and the shrubs grew larger and thicker. They stopped once to eat, and hid once when Coorah spotted birds circling high above them.

"What kind of trees are those?" Coorah asked, pointing ahead.

"Just tell me they don't have toxic wasp hairs," Gee muttered. "Whoever heard of a hairy tree?"

Darel peered toward a sparse wood rising from the plain ahead. The trees did look weird. He looked closer and realized that half the branches weren't branches at all: They were curling slides and slanted planks and rope bridges.

"That's it!" Coorah said, leaping ahead. "The possum village!"

Gee bounded past. "I bet they'll give us lolli-possums!"

"There's no such thing as lol—" Darel started.

Then he gave up and raced after them, feeling a glimmer of hope. Maybe the possums would listen. Maybe he'd finally find some allies.

He cleared a wide bush in a single leap, then leaped again, even farther. That time, at the top of his jump, he caught a better view of the possum village nestled in the woods.

Braided ropes and curved planks linked dozens of trees together, forming stairs and swings and seesaws. Ropes trailed to the ground and dangled in leaf-strewn garden paths. Darel caught a glimpse of flowers and herbs and fat seedpods growing in clumps between tree roots, and relief welled up in his chest. Anyone with such pretty gardens *had* to be friendly!

Then Coorah gave a croak of alarm and jumped sideways, one hand in her herb pouch.

Darel swerved with her, his relief suddenly turning to worry. When he reached Coorah, she was kneeling beside a lump of fur. A possum, lying motionless in the dirt.

Coorah crushed herbs in front of the possum's nose. "She's not responding."

"Wh-wh-what do you mean?" Gee asked as Coorah pressed her ear to the possum's furry chest.

Darel held his breath. *Please, please, let the possum be okay.*

Coorah shook her head and whispered, "She's dead."

"We . . . we have to tell the village," Darel said, his throat tight. "Her family."

The orange light of sunset spread across the tree-tops as they hopped toward the village in silence.

Then Gee gasped in horror. He'd found another limp possum on the ground.

"They're all dead," Ponto said as he dropped from one of the rooftop planks. "Nothing's left alive."

"There isn't a mark on them," Coorah said, kneeling beside a burly young possum sprawled across a tree root.

"How did they die? Was it nightcasting?" Gee asked, rubbing his teary eyes.

"Either that or . . ." Coorah shoved her finger pads into the possum's armpits and started wiggling them. *"This."*

"Coorah!" Gee gasped. "What're you—?"

"Stop!" the burly possum suddenly yelped, curling and giggling. "Stop, stop! I'm ticklish!"

Darel clutched his heart and Gee scrambled backward, yelling, *"Aaaah!* Possum zombie!"

"They're faking!" Coorah said, straightening. "All of them!"

The burly possum gave a bashful smile. "Sorry. We didn't know if you were friends or foes."

Dizzy with relief, Darel flopped down on a tree root and stared wide-eyed as "dead" possums started yawning and stretching and rubbing their eyes with their tails.

"After *that* trick?" Gee scoffed at the burly possum. "We're definitely foes."

"You can't blame us for that. We thought you were scorpions."

"Do we look like scorpions?"

"No, but they've been sniffing around lately, looking for our water hole."

"You have a water hole?" Gee said, finally smiling. "Then I guess you can't be all bad."

The possum twirled his tail forward to shake Gee's hand. "Why don't you stay for dinner—and all the water you can drink?"

A young possum with a fuzzy face galloped closer and beamed at Darel. "Did we really fool you? Did we? Really?"

"You really did," Darel admitted.

"I never played dead before!" the fuzzy possum said, looking from Darel to Coorah. "Not for real. I was so afraid I'd sneeze. You want to see the village?"

"We'd love to," Coorah replied.

The fuzzy possum bounded ahead of them to a swaying staircase that spiraled around a tree trunk. He scampered into the branches, then showed them the slatted walkways and the slides and ropes and ladders.

"Arabanoo would love this," Coorah said, her lips curling into a smile.

"It's tree frog heaven," Darel agreed.

Some of the possums took an hour to wake up, but eventually everyone crowded around a hanging fire pit in the center of the tree-branch village. Darel sat on a swinging bench beside Coorah, who was talking with a gray-furred possum herbalist. Happy yelps sounded from overhead, where Ponto was chasing a dozen young possums through the branches in some crazy game of tag. Darel saw that only the youngest possums hung from their tails; the older ones used theirs as spare hands.

Darel didn't say much that night; he mostly watched and listened. Partly because he still felt bad that he hadn't convinced the trapdoor spiders to fight for the Amphibilands, and partly because he wanted to do better with the possums. But mostly because he kept thinking, *It takes all kinds*. The possums were nothing like frogs, and the trapdoor spiders were even more different—and yet they both reminded Darel of home.

He slept in a hammock stretched between two branches, and when he awoke, he wandered through the tree-root gardens, sniffing the flowers and eating the occasional bee.

"Don't eat too many!" An older possum named Nioka looked up from weeding a patch of bush bananas. "Bees are a gardener's best friend."

"Sorry." Darel looked at the rows of herbs. "Did you grow all this?"

"Most of it. I love mucking around in the dirt. It's peaceful." Nioka plucked a small banana and offered it to Darel. "Do you want a bite? We eat these raw when they're young, and cook the older ones in—"

A patch of herbs rustled, and two little furballs with long tails burst through and scampered toward Darel. It was the fuzzy possum with a friend.

"Want to come to the water hole?" the fuzzy one asked Darel. "You've never seen so much wet!"

"He's a *frog*, fur-face," his friend said. "He's splashed more water than we've ever sniffed."

"So much for peaceful," Nioka said, shaking his head in amusement. "You'd better go with them, or they'll never stop asking."

Darel smiled at the young possums. "I'd love to."

He followed them along a cobbled path that curved from the trees into a shady glade at the bottom of a hill. The cobbles ended at a scattering of saplings. The water still wasn't in sight. As the little possums raced ahead, Darel crouched down and rubbed some dirt between his finger pads.

"What're you doing?" the fuzzy one said, looking back at him.

"I think the water used to reach this high."

"No way!"

Darel nodded. "Probably not all that long ago."

The fuzzy possum grabbed his hand. "Well, there's still plenty of water. I'll show you!"

Three hops later, Darel spotted the water hole. More of a puddle, really. The little ones grabbed buckets with their tails, filled them, and scampered home, leaving Darel squatting beside the puddle. He pressed his hand into the damp soil, making an imprint with his fingers, then watched the mud seep back into place.

"You're right," Nioka said from behind him. "The water hole used to be bigger. Much bigger."

Darel turned. "What happened?"

"We don't know," Nioka told him. "When I was a joey, the water welled up from the bottom every spring and refilled the hole, no matter how much of it we used."

"That doesn't happen anymore?" Darel asked.

"Not for a long time." Nioka's muzzle wrinkled with worry. "And now it's drying up completely."

Darel looked at the puddle. "What happens if you run out?"

"We'll have to move," Nioka said with a sad smile. "I don't know how, and I don't know where, but without water we can't stay here."

"There's plenty of water in the Amphibi-lands—" Darel started. "Wait, do you have a chief or something?"

Nioka smiled. "Just me, this month."

"You're the chief?" Darel cocked his head. "What do you mean, 'this month'?"

"We switch chiefs every month. That way nobody gets stuck with the job for too long."

Darel inflated his throat thoughtfully. "So are you the one I should talk to about some big news?"

"Talk to all of us."

Nioka assembled the possums in a hanging amphitheater at the center of the woods, and Darel asked Coorah to tell the story of the Amphibilands, the Veil, and Lord Marmoo. He thought maybe she'd do a better job than he had.

But before she was halfway done, Nioka stopped

her. "Wait! Wait, wait! Are you going to ask us to fight against *scorpions*?"

Coorah ducked her head in embarrassment, so Darel said, "Yes, we are."

"Do we look like warriors?" Nioka asked, gesturing behind him toward all the furry snouts and big soft ears. "Why do you think we play dead?"

"With your water running out," Darel told him, "you won't be *playing* for much longer."

The crowd shifted uneasily, and Gee's burly friend said, "The frog's got a point."

"Maybe so," an older possum grumbled, "but his point isn't as sharp as a scorpion's."

"We're asking you to join us," Darel told them. "To share our land, to share our water, to share our future. And yes—to stand with us against the scorpion army."

Nioka scratched his chin with his tail. "We heard that the scorpion lord is more powerful than ever."

"That's true," Darel admitted. "Marmoo has turned into a . . . a monster."

The crowd murmured, and a few joeys clung tighter to their parents.

"Do you have a plan to beat him?" Nioka asked.

"Yes," Darel said. "Our plan is to travel the outback

and find allies—find *friends*—who will beat him with us. We think that's what the Rainbow Serpent wants. For all of us to join together."

"I'm sorry," Nioka told him in a gentle voice. "But you'll have to keep traveling, and keep looking. We can't help you."

14

THE AFTERNOON LIGHT FILTERED through the leaves above Darel as he messed with his bag. He kept his head down, pretending that he was busy packing instead of blinking back tears. So much for his plan. So much for allies and so much for faith.

"We're leaving?" Gee asked, strolling closer and chomping on a bunya nut.

"Yeah," Darel said, scowling at his pack. "The possums didn't exactly promise to fight—"

"They did the opposite, actually," Coorah said, looking up from her pack, now overflowing with possum medicines. "They promised to keel over."

Gee gave a wry grin. "At least they gave us food."

"All the bandages I can carry," Coorah said.

"It's like they're expecting us to get wiped out."

"True," Coorah said. "But look at *this*!" She held up a pot full of bright blue muck. "How awesome is that?"

"That's not awesome," Gee said. "That's mud."

"It's blue clay," she told him. "For sucking poison from stings."

"So now you'll want me to get poisoned," Gee said, "to give you a chance to practice."

"Well . . . ," she said with a grin.

Gee snorted and looked to Darel. "Where to next?"

Darel pulled the drawstring of his bag tight and didn't answer.

"Good question," Ponto said, dropping from the treetops.

"The crayfish?" Coorah asked. "The cock-roaches? The birds?"

Darel felt his face flush. "I don't know!" he snapped. "How am I supposed to know?"

"Well," Gee said, "you're the one the Rainbow Serpent told—"

"To lower the Veil?" Darel interrupted. "Yeah, I know. So now I *also* have to decide where we go next? Who we beg for help next? Who refuses us next? Why me?"

He kicked his pack. The Veil protected the frogs, but it also cut them off from the outback—which meant they didn't *know* anyone. The trapdoor spiders said no. The possums said no. Who next? And why were Gee and Coorah and Ponto still *looking* at him? "I didn't ask for any of this!" he croaked angrily. "I'm not even a Kulipari. It's not *fair*!"

Coorah stood, and Darel expected her to scold him, but she said, "It's *totally* not fair."

"We should be back in the woods," Gee said and gave a faint grin. "*Playing* Kulipari and Scorpions."

"And getting scratches," Coorah added, "that require immediate treatment."

"You're all weirdos," Ponto muttered.

Gee draped one arm around Darel's shoulders. "We know you don't want this, D. We know you didn't ask for it."

"But you got it," Coorah told him.

"Lucky me."

"Lucky *us*," Ponto said. "You're a good leader, Darel."

"Not as good as Burnu, though," Gee teased. "*He'd* tell us where to go."

Darel snorted. Fine, if everyone thought of him as a leader, he'd better pretend he knew what he was doing. "Let's talk to the crayfish. Marmoo's got armored troops. We need some, too."

—✻—

When Yabber arrived on the outskirts of the frog village, he started telling the apprentices about Chief Olba. "She was a wise frog, and tough as an old-timer's shell." He sighed, remembering the chief's sacrifice. "But now . . . Yes, well. Let's find Old Jir, then. Used to be a Kulipari, you know. Not just any Kulipari, either . . ."

He rambled on as he led the others through the salt marsh to Jir's stump, but the old frog wasn't home. Yabber found him in a meadow beside the eucalyptus forest, standing on a platform woven of buffel grass, watching bullfrog soldiers charge a row of saplings. For a moment, Yabber thought the saplings were weighed down with fruit, unripe bay cherries or satinash apricots. Then he realized the "fruit" was actually tree frogs.

With a sudden shout, the tree frogs leaped at the bullfrogs, tongues flashing too quickly for Yabber's eyes to follow. A few of the bullfrogs gave deep ribbits of surprise, but the rest jabbed with their padded spears. A moment later, the field was writhing with battling frogs—a sea of tongues and legs and bulging throats.

The whole thing looked terribly fierce to Yabber as he stepped beside Jir.

The old frog didn't seem to agree. He shook his head sadly and declared, "Sloppy." Then he raised his voice and croaked, "Watch your flank, bullfrogs! And tree frogs, watch your ani!"

"What's an ani?" Yabber asked.

Old Jir blinked at him. "A what?"

"An ani! You told them, 'Watch your ani.'"

A crash sounded in the battlefield as a huge bullfrog, almost Ponto's size, suddenly bulldozed through the tree frog ranks. Tongues shot wildly into the air around her, tree frogs cascaded into the air like popworms popping, and the huge bullfrog laughed as she slugged the "enemy" in every direction.

"Watch *Orani*," Old Jir explained. "The bullfrog princess."

"I didn't even know they had princesses."

"Bullfrog royalty keep to themselves." Old Jir gestured toward the rampaging bullfrog. "And do *you* want to tell her she's not a princess?"

"No, no! I shrink into my shell at the thought!" Yabber watched for a moment. "She seems to be quite . . . enjoying herself."

"She does, doesn't she?" Old Jir said, then raised his voice. "Orani! Look behind you!"

The big bullfrog princess turned and grinned at the trail of destruction behind her. "Just gettin' started!" she croaked.

"In the wrong direction," Old Jir told her. "You're trying to capture the sapling before the tree frogs capture your puddle."

"Oops!" Orani called out cheerily, and started bulldozing in the other direction.

Old Jir sighed. "She makes *Darel* look level-headed." His white eyes shifted toward the dream-caster apprentices. "So . . . this is the wrecking crew? Here to tear down the Veil?"

Yabber nodded. "Yes."

Old Jir watched the mock battle for a moment. "When do you start?"

"We already have."

"Dreamcasting." Old Jir snorted. "I forget that it looks exactly like standing around." He paused for a moment before continuing. "How long before the Veil comes down?"

"Unwinding a casting as powerful as the turtle king's is tricky," Yabber explained. "We'll work slowly and steadily, unfurling the Veil one strand at a time, until all of a sudden, in the blink of an eye, the entire thing will fall."

"And then the age of peace is over."

"It's already over." Yabber gazed toward the battlefield. "At least the frogs look ready."

"But they're not," Old Jir told him.

15

PONTO BULGED HIS EYES AT SOMETHING Darel couldn't see, then raised his fist to his shoulder, indicating to the other frogs to stop.

"*Pssst,*" Darel hissed to Coorah and Gee, and then he crept up beside Ponto, who'd crouched down behind a thistle bush.

"There," Ponto whispered, nodding toward the rock-strewn field ahead.

For a moment, Darel didn't see anything but piles of jagged stones. Then he noticed faint paths on the dusty ground, and realized he was looking at a village. The scattered rocks formed little stony houses— sloped roofs, craggy walls, pebbled patios—but nothing moved.

"Geckos," Ponto said. "Except . . . they're gone."

"Maybe they're playing dead, too," Gee said.

"They don't do that," Ponto told him. "They drop their tails if they're threatened. They don't just disappear."

When Darel headed closer to the gecko village, the buildings reminded him a little of the Amphibilands' leaf villages, except low and stony. Then he saw them: hundreds of jagged marks perforating the dry, dusty ground.

"Scorpion tracks," Coorah whispered.

"Gee, hop onto a roof and keep your eyes peeled." Darel scanned the village. "Coorah, look for any sign of life—any geckos who might need you."

"What're you going to do?"

"I'm going to follow these tracks."

He stalked through the stony ghost town, back-tracking a few times but finally stopping outside a flat, sprawling rock that covered a craggy hole in the earth. He sniffed at the darkness. It smelled moist. He squeezed under the rock, then blinked until his eyes adjusted to the darkness.

"What is it?" Ponto asked behind him.

Darel jerked in surprise and whacked his head on the rock. "It's the geckos' water hole," he said, rubbing his sore spot. "Empty now. And look at the tracks."

Ponto grunted. "Scorps in and out, over and over."

"Scooping up all the water," Darel told him, "and dragging it off."

"So what happened to the lizards? There aren't any bodies."

Darel shook his head. "Either they ran off or . . . Marmoo took them."

"Took them? Why?"

"I don't know," Darel said. "But it can't be good."

The next day, the midday sun burned bright and harsh on the outback. Brown twigs crackled under tender toe pads, scratchy shrubs dotted the parched earth, and the air seemed to suck the moisture from Darel's skin.

"I need a water break," Gee croaked.

"Once we reach those trees," Ponto said, nodding toward the horizon.

Darel blinked his stinging eyes toward the acacias in the distance. "Looks good. Shade."

"Too far," Gee grumped. "My skin's going to peel off halfway there."

Darel slitted his nostrils as a hot wind blew from the east. Sand stung his skin and dry, pointy-edged leaves swirled past, occasionally jabbing him or— judging from the occasional grunt—Coorah or Gee. Or Ponto. But of course the big Kulipari refused to admit that flying vegetation could hurt him.

They hopped for hours, until even Gee was too tired to keep grumbling. The distant acacias didn't seem to get any closer, and Darel almost worried that the trees were a mirage—except that everyone else saw them, too. So he kept his mouth shut and staggered onward, over the burning sand, under the scorching sun.

Coorah made them stop twice to sprinkle the last of the water from the possum village on their skin. Finally, as the sun turned orange and sank toward the horizon, they reached the first cluster of acacia trees.

They flopped down in the shade, not too close to the thorny trunk of the tree, and Ponto unstrapped a waterskin that had a wide mouth. He passed it to Coorah, and she dunked her head inside for a minute before giving it to Gee, who did the same.

"How much farther to the crayfish?" Gee asked, his skin now glossy again. He passed the waterskin to Darel.

"Don't they need rivers or lakes?" Coorah asked, scanning the horizon. "I don't see any water."

"Some of them live in swamps," Ponto replied.

"Some in the rain forest, some in the button-grass fields. We're not looking for any old crayfish—we're looking for *burrowing* crayfish."

"They actually tunnel?"

"Yep," Ponto ribbited. "Old Jir says they live in underground mazes, and all you can see of their villages are lumpy chimneys sticking up from the ground. They've got two big claws, and a curving tail—"

"Like scorps?" Gee asked.

"A little. But their tails curve downward—and don't sting."

"How many legs?"

"Eight."

Gee narrowed his eyes in suspicion. "Do they have carapaces?"

"Sort of."

Darel grinned as he rubbed a few beads of water into his skin. He knew where this was going.

"Wait a minute," Gee said. "Are they *arachnids*?"

"Nah," Ponto said. "Crustaceans."

"Which are what, exactly?"

Ponto stretched out in the shade. "A kind of arthropod."

"So are arachnids! We're killing ourselves crossing

this deathscape to beg a bunch of *arachnids* for help?"

"They're not arachnids," Ponto said.

"Arachnids, arthropods—same thing."

"You're an amphibian," Coorah told Gee, "and so are salamanders, but that doesn't make you a salamander."

"There's no such thing as a salamander," Gee scoffed.

Darel closed his eyes, and Coorah's and Gee's soft croaking faded into the background murmur of the outback—the whisper of the dry wind and the faltering song of an occasional cricket. Rough-edged leaves shook in the breeze, until the dry rustling turned into the splashing of water . . .

Darel found himself standing neck-deep in a spreading pond, with the acacia trees looming high above. Except he wasn't standing. He was swimming. And he didn't have any legs. For a moment, he panicked. Then he saw three other pollywogs swimming around him. Coorah, Gee, and Ponto splashing and jumping in this nursery pool in the middle of the outback.

Time to turn into frogs, a voice said. *And hop into the big wide world.*

"We're not ready!" Tadpole Gee cried.

Tadpole Coorah shook her head. "Not yet!"

You can't stay in the nursery forever, the voice said.

"Just a little longer?" Tadpole Ponto asked. "It's not safe out there!"

It's not safe, the voice agreed. *You're changing; you're growing. From egg to tadpole to frog. You cannot hide forever without denying your nature. You must leave this protected place.*

"Now?" Darel heard himself ask.

Yes, the voice said. *The time is now.*

The pond shimmered with a hundred colors, which swirled together into a brilliant rainbow that arched over a giant red rock tower. As the rainbow spread, Darel realized that the tower was enormous, the size of a mountain, standing alone in an endless plain.

"What is that?" he asked.

The tadpoles were gone. The voice was silent.

"What's that red rock?" he asked again.

Raindrops dotted the surface of the pond, blurring the images. Just a drizzle, at first, then a sudden downpour. *Pock, pock, pock.* The rainbow broke apart into a thousand shards—

—and Darel awoke.

He blinked at the darkness under the trees. There was no pool of water, no rainbow light. Night had fallen while he'd slept, and Gee's faint, familiar snore sounded nearby.

As did a soft *pock*, *pock* . . .

Darel peered at the stars dotting the sky. There weren't any clouds, though the noise sounded like raindrops in the leaves overhead. *Pock. Pock.* Whatever that was, it wasn't rain.

16

THE SOFT SAND UNDERFOOT MADE Pigo's stomach twist uncomfortably. He was born to skitter across hard rock and real sand—dry sand—not this saltwater mushiness. Every step sickened him. If he couldn't depend on sand, what *could* he depend on?

By habit, his side eyes shifted toward the moonlit silhouette ahead of him. But no, he couldn't depend on his lordship. Not anymore. The scorpion lord—though he called himself the king now—hadn't been the same since Queen Jarrah cast her spell on him. Almost as if he had shed not just his carapace but his *self*.

Still, Pigo obeyed him, crossing the stomach-churning sand, with the endless thunder of the surf in his ears. The ocean . . . Pigo shuddered. Worse than a wasteland. Undrinkable water, as far as the eye could see.

"Here!" Lord Marmoo called. "Pigo!"

Pigo hustled closer. Though not too close, because Lord Marmoo stood with his feet actually in the surf. He didn't even seem to notice the water lapping and swirling around him.

"Yes, my lord," he said.

"King," Lord Marmoo corrected, the moonlight glinting on his scarred face.

"My king," Pigo repeated, feeling the twist in his stomach again.

Lord Marmoo swept a pincer toward the waves. "What do you see, little brother?"

"The end of the world," Pigo said, staring at the ocean. "Land we can't conquer and water we can't drink."

"The last time we attacked the Amphibilands," Lord Marmoo told him, "the frogs were saved by reinforcements coming across the water."

"The turtles and the Kulipari," Pigo said, nodding.

"That won't happen again," Lord Marmoo said with a sharp edge in his voice. "Not this time." Then he turned and faced the ocean . . . and crouched.

"My lord, don't!" Pigo said, reaching out to stop him.

Too late. Marmoo leaped from the shallows, higher and farther than any normal scorpion.

Again Pigo shouted. "No! My lord!" He spun toward the scorpion squad standing higher on the beach, well away from the tide, his mind whirling with outlandish plans to rescue Lord Marmoo from the sea.

Then he heard Lord Marmoo's laughter from the dark waves. He turned back and saw the impossible: A stone's throw from the beach, Marmoo was *standing on the water,* his legs half-submerged but his abdomen above the surface.

"H-h-huh . . . how?" Pigo stammered.

Lord Marmoo lifted a mid-leg above the water, then stomped down with it. "I'm on the reef."

Pigo exhaled in relief, though he didn't know if he was more relieved that Marmoo wasn't drowning or that Marmoo didn't actually have the ability to stroll across water.

Out on the reef, Marmoo turned to face the ocean. "I am King Marmoo!" he shouted.

The only answer Pigo heard was the crash of waves.

"You will serve me," Marmoo continued, "or I will smash your reef to rubble. I'll destroy your hunting grounds."

Pigo thought he caught a flash of movement in the water beyond Marmoo, but he wasn't sure.

"Your pups will go hungry," Marmoo threatened. "And when I'm done with this one, I will crush every reef off the coast until you obey!"

He lashed with his stinger at the reef, sending up a spew of salt water and chunks of coral. Then he struck again and again, his tail plunging deeper into the ocean as he tore the reef to shreds. The frothing water rose to his underbelly as he destroyed the reef directly beneath himself.

Pigo watched in horror. Was Marmoo so intent on destruction that he'd drown himself in this lashing frenzy? "M-m-my lord," he said too softly to be heard.

Suddenly, Marmoo stopped lashing at the reef and turned toward the ocean. He cocked his head and seemed to be listening. And this time, Pigo was *sure* that he saw shapes moving among the crests and troughs of the moonlit sea. Strange, flat, bat-like shapes gliding underwater.

"Turtle soldiers will try to come past your reefs," Marmoo told the ocean. "They'll be swimming for the Amphibilands, to help the frogs. And when they do, you will stop them."

A watery gurgle sounded from beyond Marmoo.

"I don't care if you fight them," Marmoo said. "Just stop them."

Pigo didn't hear the rest of the conversation over the pounding surf, but finally Marmoo turned toward the beach and leaped again. He fell short, and for a moment disappeared in the water—everything except his stinger. Then he jumped again, bursting from the surf.

He landed beside Pigo, dripping foul seawater, his carapace draped with ropy green weeds. "It's done," he told Pigo. "The stingrays are mine to command."

"Stingrays? I heard they're gentle creatures."

"They're weak and soft," Lord Marmoo scoffed, his disfigured face horrible in the moonlight. "But they'll do what they're told, to save their pups."

"And now, my lord . . . king?"

"We rejoin the horde. And the moment the Veil falls, we attack."

AREL LAY BACK AND LISTENED TO the sound of the waterless rain, thinking about his dream. Not just a dream: a message from the Rainbow Serpent. But what did it mean, *The time is now*? And, *You must leave this protected place*? Leave the Amphibilands? That was even worse than lowering the Veil. So what did the dream mean? Was the Veil falling right now? It couldn't be—not yet. He was in the middle of the outback! He hadn't found a single ally.

"You awake?" he whispered to nobody in particular.

Gee gave a louder snore, and Coorah said, "I've got an herb for that."

"You ever hear about a huge red rock tower in the middle of the outback?" Darel asked, hoping to "accidentally" wake someone up. "I mean, seriously huge, like an entire mountain—"

Pock–pock–pock–pock! The sound grew louder,

coming from the leaves above. Then a rain of round black shapes fell from the branches and landed on the ground with a thud. Some were as big as Darel's fist, and each one had two rows of wiggling legs, and sharp, bloodsucking snouts.

"Wake up!" Darel croaked, leaping to his feet. "There are things! *Things!*"

"*Ch-ch-ch,*" one of the black shapes chattered. "Not *ch*-things."

Gee was on his feet and standing back-to-back with Darel before he'd even finished his snore.

"I was sleeping," Coorah grumped. Then her eyes bulged when she saw the black shapes creeping closer. "Are those ticks?"

"*Paralysis* ticks." Ponto sprang to his feet. "Don't let them bite you."

"Unlike all those other things," Gee murmured sarcastically, "that you *do* want to bite you."

"Bite chu," a tick chattered. "Bite, bite *chu*."

Pock pock pock. More ticks fell from the trees, *pock*ing the leaves before hitting the ground. They wriggled their tiny legs in the air until they managed to turn right side up. "*Ch*-tasty," they said, crawling for the frogs. "Sweet *ch*-blood, fresh-*ch* blood."

Darel pulled his dagger, eyeing the oncoming swarm.

"My gram used to use them in surgery," Coorah said, grabbing her fighting stick. "If they inject you, you'll freeze up. One bite, you can't move your arm. Three bites, you can't walk."

"Then they can take their time," Ponto said grimly, "draining your blood."

Gee groaned, and the ticks crawled closer in a chittering tide.

"Stay together," Ponto said, backing away. "They're mean, but they're slow."

Darel kept his dagger high as he and the others followed Ponto deeper into the stand of acacias. The ticks crept after them, heads waving in the air . . . but they *were* slow. Too slow. They'd never catch a frog like this. So why were they all advancing from one direction?

What if the ticks weren't *attacking* them? What if the ticks were *herding* them?

"Stop!" Darel blurted. "Wait! They're moving us toward the trees, it's an ambu—"

Pockpockpockpockpock! Dozens of ticks pelted at them from above, in a bloodsucking deluge.

"I'm on it," Ponto shouted, and he leaped straight upward into the branches.

"*Ya!*" Darel yelped when a tick landed on his shoulder.

He flicked the tick away, but another crawled onto his foot. Coorah smacked the tick with her fighting stick, and Darel grunted in pain, then slapped her knee, doing the same for her. For a few terrified moments, the only sound was the "*ch-ch-ch*" of the ticks and the desperate grunting and slapping of the frogs.

Then Gee gasped. "I'm bit! My leg!"

Darel spun to find Gee dragging his left leg as he desperately fended off three ticks, his nostrils flared and his eyes narrow.

Coorah yelped, "Darel! I'm—"

Coorah flopped to the ground in front of him. Her eyes blinked furiously, but the rest of her was perfectly motionless.

"*Ch-Darel*?" a bloated tick said. "The frog-*ch* that King Marmoo-*ch* hates most?"

"Marmoo's not a king," Gee snarled, smacking another tick away. "He's a maniac."

"*Him!*" the bloated tick said, eyeing Darel. "Get that one-*ch*. Ch. Ch. Bite him."

Darel dragged Coorah toward Gee, who was tilting to one side because of his frozen leg. "We've got to get out of here," Darel said, his voice urgent. "Can you walk?"

"Of course I can walk," Gee said, and fell onto his face.

With a whimper, Darel jumped in front of the advancing tide of ticks, and shouted to the tree-tops, "Ponto! A little help?"

"*Ch*-him!" the ticks cried. "Darel! *Ch!* Get him!"

The ticks crept over tree roots and weeds, churning closer, and Darel spun in a tight circle, slashing with his dagger. Then—*finally*—Ponto dropped from the tree and landed in front of him!

Relief sparked in Darel's heart . . . until Ponto collapsed onto his side, as still as a statue. Totally paralyzed.

"Oh, fungus," Darel said.

The ticks jumped him.

His dagger slashed at them in a blur. He crouched, he kicked, he spun—he tore through the first five ticks, the next ten. But they kept coming. Three ticks landed on his arm, and when he brushed them away, others bit his leg and knee.

He slammed to the ground, unable to move, staring upward in helpless horror as more ticks fell from the acacia leaves onto his face. Pain flared when they bit his cheeks and forehead. Once, twice—five times. A dead numbness spread across his skin, his eyes barely opened, his mouth frozen in a twisted grimace.

It was over. The ticks had won. Darel and the others were going to die out here.

Then a yellow glow touched the branches over-head, and Darel heard Ponto saying, "You're not the only ones with poison."

He'd tapped his Kulipari power, and burned the tick poison from his veins. The yellow glow shifted on the leaves, and battered ticks started flinging past as Ponto smashed them. Darel's vision blurred—and then turned completely black.

Darel felt something cool on his face. A goopy tingle spread across his cheeks and forehead. He managed to open his eyes just enough to see Coorah kneeling over him, painting his face with bright blue clay.

Over her shoulder, the acacia trees glowed completely yellow, and Darel's heart squeezed tight. Ponto was tapping way too deeply into his poison! He'd burn himself out, and turn white and weak like Old Jir.

Then Darel realized that the yellow glow was coming from the sunrise. He'd slept all night. He tried to smile, but his lips only twitched.

"How does that feel?" Coorah asked.

"Mmph," he told her.

"You sound better already," she told him.

"Ooh and Eee?" he asked.

"Me and Gee? I already treated us." She showed him two blue smears on her skin. "See?"

"Ooh-ari."

"What?"

"Ooh. Ooh-ari."

"I have no idea what you're saying." She applied another layer of clay to Darel's face. "Go back to sleep. You'll feel better when you wake up."

"No seep," he slurred. "Guh stay wake."

"Fine," she said. "Stay awake, then. But first check that you're strong enough to close your eyes all the way."

On the third try, Darel managed to close his eyes all the way . . . and immediately fell asleep.

"Darel!" Gee's voice sounded urgent. "Can you move?"

Darel awoke, his heart hammering, to find Gee shaking his shoulder.

"Can you blink?" Gee asked.

"Can." He took a breath. "Talk."

"Great! Blink once if you want the good news, twice if you want the terrible news." Without waiting for a blink, Gee continued, "The good news is, your face will be okay in a few minutes."

"Waz the turbil newz?"

"You're not going to live that long." Gee pulled Darel into a seated position and pointed to the sky. "Birds of prey."

A dozen huge, terrifying birds circled in the air above the acacia trees. Beaks sharp, talons wickedly curved. Each wing as long as Darel from head to toe pad.

"They're here to finish what the ticks started," Coorah said.

18

PIPPI SAT ON HER HAUNCHES IN THE deepest chamber of the new Stargazer burrow, gazing at the candlelit wall. Condensation trickled down the uneven rock, collected in cracks, and dripped to the floor. She thought about the weight of the dirt above her, and watched one droplet drip to a jutting edge of quartz.

The droplet hung there, about to fall. It shivered and danced, growing rounder and fuller . . . but didn't drop.

"Do you see anything?" her sister, Pirra, asked from the entrance.

Pippi shook her head. "I'm not a Stargazer, Pirra."

"Not *yet*. But as long as the real one is off hibernating, you're the closest thing we have."

"Don't even say that!" Pippi curled her bill in embarrassment. "When the Stargazer wakes up, she's going to love this new dripping room."

Pirra eyed her. "Even if she wakes up anytime soon,

she can't get into the Amphibilands. C'mon, let's head home."

Pippi followed Pirra through the tunnels to the burrow mouth and blinked at the midday sun. She heard the distant clash of frog squads practicing military maneuvers, and the even more distant clamor of construction as other frogs strengthened the defenses.

Even though the new Stargazer burrow was a long way from the village, Pippi wasn't surprised to see platypuses swimming in the river when she pushed through the concealing curtain of vines. She'd organized platypus patrols all through the rivers and streams of the Amphibilands, so when the scorpions attacked, the platypuses would know the lay of the land. Or the way of the water.

But her bill tingled when she realized that the shapes gliding through the water weren't platypuses. "Turtles!" she yelped in pleasure. "Yabber!"

Yabber and three other turtles swam with slow grace toward the burrow. They clambered onto the shore, and Yabber stretched his long neck toward her. "There you are, Okipippi! We've been looking for you."

"How was your trip? Is everything okay?"

"Why were you looking for her?" Pirra asked.

"Because she's the Stargazer's star pupil." Yabber furrowed his brow. "Which rather makes her a star star-gazer pupil, now that I think about it."

Pirra blinked. "Huh?"

"I mean to say," Yabber explained, "if she's the Stargazer's star pupil, she's got two 'stars' then a 'gazer' and a 'pupil' . . ." He trailed off at Pirra's blank gaze, and turned to Pippi. "If you follow my meaning."

"I kind of don't," she admitted.

"Because he's not making any sense." Pirra looked to Yabber. "When will the turtle soldiers get here?"

"The shelled regiments are on the way," Yabber told her. "They don't move fast, though."

"And when will you finish, you know"—Pirra wrinkled her bill—"taking down the Veil?"

"We've been unraveling it for days." Yabber gave a sad smile. "We're ready to remove one more strand of dreamcasting right now, perhaps the last one . . . if your sister agrees."

"*Me?*" Pippi squeaked, shifting her weight off her knuckles. "I don't know, Yabber. Why can't we just stay inside the Veil forever?"

"Some things," he told her, "are not meant to be."

Pippi thwapped her tail unhappily. That wasn't a reason! That wasn't an answer! That was just a way of *not* answering. What was she supposed to say? Why *her*? She didn't know anything about any of this!

"But Darel and Gee are still out there."

"He told me not to wait."

"And Ponto and Coorah!" Pippi curled her bill. "And they're looking for allies, and we don't have any yet!"

"Darel told me to have faith."

"That doesn't mean we're in a crazy rush!"

Yabber furrowed his brow. "The Rainbow Serpent told him to lower the Veil. Not to wait around and *eventually* lower the Veil. He made me promise to lower it as soon as possible. But you're the Stargazer's pupil. I cannot make this decision alone."

Pippi frowned. She didn't want to do this. She didn't want to change everything. Why couldn't the Veil just stay? Why couldn't things stop changing all the time?

Then the soft plunk of a drop of water hitting rock echoed through the burrow, and the memory of that fat droplet in the dripping wall sprang to her mind. The flowing of water was a kind of change, too. What if the droplet had refused to fall? What if it had been too afraid?

Water had to flow. From the clouds, from the

mountains, from the springs. Water had to flow—even if that meant flowing away forever.

"Okay." Pippi took a breath. "Remove the last strand."

Yabber closed his eyes as the golden glow of his dreamcasting touched the Veil. Seeping into the magical dome, gentle and firm. He felt the apprentices working alongside him, tugging at the old king's knotted strands of power. He felt the great Veil looming above, like the sheltering canopy of an ancient tree. Full of life, a safe haven from the ills of the outback.

Then a chill of fear touched him. He was about to expose the frogs to all those ills, to all those dangers.

Taking a calming breath, he imagined the Rainbow Serpent rising from a mountain pool. He needed to have faith. He needed to trust the Serpent. He hoped he was doing the right thing. He hoped he was saving the frogs, not destroying them.

His dreamcasting unfurled high above him, and he felt the Veil begin to crumble.

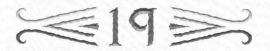

19

WHEN PIGO FOLLOWED KING Marmoo to the top of the hill, he felt his heart beat in awe. His side eyes saw the ghost bats wheeling in the air, the lizards massed behind the caged geckos, the legions of spiders—including Lady Fahlga with her nightcasters—and the endless columns of battle-hardened scorpion troops.

"This isn't the mightiest horde *since* the days of legend . . . ," Pigo said, his main eyes scanning the assembled warriors.

King Marmoo turned his ruined face to Pigo, his mouthparts shifting into a sneer. "What did you say, Commander?"

". . . it's the mightiest horde *including* the days of legend," Pigo finished.

With a satisfied grunt, King Marmoo scanned the dry scrubland. "Now we must trust that the spider was correct, and the frogs are foolish enough to lower their only defense against me. If she wasn't, she'll pay the pri—"

A flash of golden light interrupted him, and there was a sound like the rustling of a million leaves.

When Pigo turned, his breath caught. The dry scrubland was gone, and the Amphibilands towered in front of him. He marveled at the gently sloping hills, the distant glint of streams, trees heavy with succulent leaves, everything lush and emerald green. The scent of the rich earth made his mouth water. Below him, the troops shouted and roared and jostled closer to the green border of the froglands.

King Marmoo raised a pincer. In two heartbeats, silence fell, broken only by the whisper of the wind and the buzz of blue-banded bees.

"These are the *new* days of legend," Marmoo called into the stillness. "You are not just fighting a battle. You are reshaping the land—you are seizing the water, and the outback will echo with your names forever."

A cheer sounded, first from the scorpions, then from the rest of the horde.

"Today," Marmoo bellowed, "the Arachnilands rise from the ashes of the Amphibilands! Today, we conquer. Today, we feast!" He lowered his pincer. "Attack!"

The army rampaged toward Pigo and King Marmoo, battalion after battalion thundering up the rise, parting around them—eyes wild, faces alight with bloodlust—then charging into the soft, helpless land behind them.

For a few long minutes, Pigo watched the first waves of the army get swallowed by the thick green walls. Then the song of battle started—shouts of fear, screams of pain, the clash of weapons—and he snapped a pincer in satisfaction.

"I'm eager to enter the fray, my king," he told Marmoo. "If you'll let me—"

"Not yet," Marmoo said. "Not until the ghost bats— Ah."

A dozen bats flitted over the trees and landed in front of Marmoo, spreading their wings in strange bows. *"We did as you commanded, my king,"* a red-eyed one said in a whispery voice.

"Past the hills," another hissed, *"past the forest and the river. That is where you'll find the biggest frog village."*

"It is heavily defended," the first said.

"That's where they'll make their final stand," Marmoo told Pigo before looking down at the bats. "And the Kulipari?"

"No sign of them."

Marmoo's ruined mouthparts moved into a smile. "Then they aren't fighting yet. When they fight, they're not exactly hard to spot. They'll come."

"And when they do?" Pigo asked.

"I'll handle them personally. Stab your squad like a dagger into the heart of the Amphibilands. Drive the frogs in front of you, push them without mercy toward this village. I want all the frogs in one place before I finish them."

Pigo saluted. "Yes, my king!"

With the red-banded scorps and elite spider archers flanking him, Pigo marched into the Amphibilands, following the trail of crushed plants and the cries of injured warriors.

DAREL WATCHED THE BIRDS OF PREY through the leaves of the acacia. Dark wings shifted in the air, and the birds tilted toward the stand of trees. With a fearful gulp, Darel turned to Ponto.

Only a Kulipari could save them now. But Ponto looked paler than usual, like he'd already tapped too deeply into his poison.

"Take cover!" Coorah called. "They're coming!"

Darel bulged his eyes as the birds swooped toward them—beautiful, majestic, and deadly.

Ponto started glowing faintly, but when the birds slashed closer through the wind, Darel whispered, "Ponto, no."

Ponto looked at him with his blackening eyes. "No?"

"No."

"You sure?"

Darel swallowed the lump in his throat. "Don't fight."

The blackness in Ponto's eyes faded. "I hope you know what you're doing."

"All I know," Gee said, "is that I'm the *first* one they're going to eat."

The birds plummeted closer. Darel saw the slits in their razor beaks and the predatory gleam in their eyes. His heart clenched as Gee, Coorah, and Ponto stood around him like a living shield . . . Then the birds struck down, slashing and biting.

Not at Darel and his friends, though. Instead, the birds started plucking paralysis ticks—who'd been warily watching Ponto from a safe distance—from the scrub and gobbling them down.

Darel slumped in relief. "Harriers," he croaked out.

"These are the harrier hawks?" Coorah asked. "The ones Pippi mentioned?"

"I don't care how hairy they are," Gee said, wiping his forehead. "As long as they're stopping the ticks from draining my blood."

The nearest hawk said, *"Keek! Kee kee keek-keek-keek-ee."*

Gee gaped at the hawk. "What?"

"Keek! Kee-ee kee!"

"Well, glad to meet you," Gee told the hawk. "I'm Gee."

"What?" Darel said. "Huh?"

"'Huh' what?" Gee asked, glancing at him. "Aren't you going to introduce yourself?" He looked back to the hawk. "That's Darel, Coorah, and the big one's Ponto."

"Kee-ee-keek?" the hawk asked.

"Nah, he's Kulipari," Gee explained. "The rest of us are wood frogs. Oh, except Darel's also . . ." He glanced at Darel's clay-smeared face again. "The Blue Face King."

"Wait, wait." Coorah blinked at Gee, inflating her throat in befuddlement. "You can understand him?"

"Kee-kee-eee!" the hawk cried. *"Kee kee."*

"She's a her," Gee told Coorah. "And sure. Can't you?"

"Uh . . . no."

"Keek ee-kee-kee!" the bird shrilled, then flapped its wings a few times.

Gee nodded to the hawk. "I know. You sound good to me."

"So you speak *bird*?" Ponto asked.

"Guess so," Gee said.

"Okay." Darel rubbed his numb face. "This is unexpected."

"Kee!" the first bird said. *"Kee-ee-kee!"*

The other birds hopped closer and started *kee*ing at Gee, who looked faintly ill.

"The Veil," he stammered when they quieted down. "The Veil has fallen."

"Already?" Darel asked, his stomach sinking. "Are they sure? How do they know?"

"Because all of a sudden, they can see the Amphibilands," Gee explained. "They never could before. And they saw Marmoo's armies heading for the Amphibilands. Scorpions, spiders, bees, bats, snakes—"

"We've got to get back," Ponto blurted, pacing in frustration. "We're days away. We can't help them; we're too far away."

Darel pushed to his feet, and limped toward the hawks, who inspected him with cold, predator eyes. "We need you," he told them. "Not just the frogs, not just the Amphibilands. The entire outback needs you. You've seen Marmoo? You've seen how he's changed?"

The birds were *kee*ing softly, and a few scratched at the earth with scaly talons.

"Yeah," Gee said. "They've seen him."

"The spider queen's nightcasting twisted Marmoo," Darel told them. "It changed him. He doesn't belong in the outback. He's not just a predator, not anymore. I wish we frogs could hide from that—I wish we could hide from him. But we *do* belong in the outback. The wallabies belong, the geckos belong. The turtles, the possums, the hawks—even the ticks and spiders and scorpions belong. We all belong. Friend and foe, prey and predator, we all belong."

The hawks watched him closely. With interest, he hoped, and not hunger.

"But not Marmoo," Darel continued, "not anymore. If he wins, he will wipe us out. The frogs, the turtles, the possums, the lizards. Until only scorpions remain. Does that sound like the outback to you? Does that sound like home?"

For a long moment, none of the hawks made a sound. Then the one who'd first spoken to Gee rattled off a series of *ee-kee-kee-ee-eek*s.

"She says they never meddle in the troubles of the earthbound," Gee explained.

Darel frowned. "So they won't join us?"

A harrier hawk shoved her razor-sharp beak close to Darel's face, and he managed not to flinch only because he was still half-paralyzed.

"Keek-ee!" the bird shrilled.

"They won't fight," Gee told Darel. "But they *will* help."

21

SCORPIONS MASSED AT THE RIVERBANK, tails curving toward Pippi, eager to strike. Bloody pincers snapped shut, and battle-crazed voices shouted threats. But they didn't wade after her—they were afraid of the water.

Pippi took a quick, gulping breath, then dove to the bottom and swam past the scorps. Above her, the surface of the river pocked and splashed as the webbing of spider archers struck the water, and she shuddered.

She'd seen one of their webs drag a platypus from the water an hour ago, and the memory still made her want to cry. But she didn't. She veered to the left, then the right, swimming faster to avoid the nets.

After a day of fighting, the scorpion army had driven the frogs from the heavily fortified Outback Hills, from the eucalyptus forest and the eastern flats. Pippi and the other platypus messengers swam the streams and rivers, bringing messages and supplies—but in the past few hours, she'd only passed along a single message: "Retreat! Back to the village!"

She'd just come from the river that flowed near the banyan trees, where the tree frogs were trying to hold off the scorpions while under attack by the ghost bats. She and Pirra had watched the terrifying flicker of white wings through the branches. They'd seen the scorpions climbing higher on the sinewy banyan tree trunks, two fresh warriors replacing every one that the tree frogs defeated.

Pippi had whacked her tail in the water and yelled, "The wood frogs are in trouble in the eucalyptus forest! They need help!"

Actually, the eucalyptus forest had fallen hours earlier. Pippi had just wanted to send the bats off on a wild-goose chase.

For a second, Pirra had stared blankly at her. Then she'd understood, and thwacked her tail, too. "Go, go! Quickly!"

"Let's finish off the frogs in the eucalyptus forest first," one ghost bat had told the others. *"Then we'll come back for these tree frogs."*

Half the ghost bats flew off, and Pirra turned to Pippi. "You fooled them. Good plan—but what now?"

"I don't know . . ." She'd paused. "Actually, wait. You stay here."

Pippi had taken a breath and pulled herself onto the riverbank. Platypuses weren't good at walking, but she'd been practicing so much that her knuckles were calloused and her legs strong. She'd shouted at the scorpions—insults that Gee had taught her—until she'd attracted the attention of the nearest squad.

"You can't even catch a platypus, you arach-nerds!" she'd yelled. "And you goggle-eyed spiders are worse!"

With a roar, they'd rushed her, and she'd reached the water an inch ahead of their pincers. But by then Pirra had joined in, shouting insults and splashing the scorps and spiders. Together, they had drawn half of the attackers to the riverbank—then Pippi had lunged from the water and slashed at a scorp with her spur. She'd missed, but her attack enraged the scorps, and in the blink of an eye, an entire mob was chasing her instead of fighting.

Behind her, Pirra had signaled for the tree frog retreat, and with half the bats and scorps gone, the frogs were able to leap from the branches into the safety of the river.

Pippi hadn't stayed to watch—she'd led the scorps away, splashing them every now and then to keep them angry.

Now she finally ditched them, swimming under-water across a pond and slipping into a side stream. As she swam closer to the main village, the stream grew crowded with frog warriors drifting in the current, drinking through their skin. Preparing to return to battle or nursing wounds—or both.

Princess Orani lifted her head from the salty water and blinked her stinging eyes. She couldn't see far through the mist of the marsh, but she heard the grumbling of a spider squad clearly enough.

"'Circle around through the swamp. Attack the village from behind,'" a spider grunted. "That's easy for the *king* to say."

"Yeah," another grumbled. "He's not the one stuck in this muck."

Orani pointed two finger pads to her left, and a soft splash sounded from behind her as her bullfrog squad moved into position. She climbed onto a weedy hillock and crouched to spring.

When the spiders crawled into sight, she shouted, "Hit 'em!"

She leaped at the spiders and tore through the front rank, losing herself in the frenzy of battle. A squad of spider archers shot webs at her while warriors slashed with swords, and through the red haze of battle she heard herself laugh as she hammered spider after spider.

She saw her squad slam into the flank of the advancing spiders, and caught a sword in the air. "You messed with the wrong princess," she said while punching a spider across the marsh.

"Orani!" one of her scouts called. "You need to see this!"

She tore a thick reed from the ground, batted two spiders away, then leaped toward her scout. "What's up?"

"Down by the coast," the scout said.

"The turtles?" she asked, feeling a glimmer of relief. "They're finally here?"

The scout shook his head. "I don't think so."

She called for her squad to follow and headed for the beach. She burst from the marsh and jumped to the coastal dunes, which were covered with dry, wavering beach grass. The ocean spread before her, the surf lapping at the sand and the water an endless field of rippling blue, glinting under the sun.

Then she gasped. "What is *that*?"

Black splotches seemed to float on the waves. A dozen of them. No, *hundreds* of black dots rising and falling with the waves. And coming closer.

She raced to the top of a dune for a better look. "Scorpions," she whispered, a chill touching her heart. She turned to her squad. "Bring the catapults to the beach—*now*!"

"They're defending the village," one of her frogs said.

"We need them here!" she bellowed. "We need every bullfrog in the Amphibilands! Move, move, *move*!"

The next few minutes dissolved into a blur of frenzied action. Orani positioned her squads and watched the scorpions draw closer. First she noticed tails and stingers above the black splotches, then pincers and mouthparts. And finally, she saw how they were crossing the ocean.

"They're riding stingrays," she said, shaking her head.

"Where are the turtles?" a bullfrog warrior asked. "Why aren't they here?"

"The turtles can't help us now." Orani scanned the dunes behind her. "Get those catapults ready!

Dune squads, stay alert. My squad—do what we always do." She howled a war cry. *"Attack!"*

She leaped forward and landed in the surf, then leaped again and landed on the nearest stingray. She heard her squad screaming the bullfrog war cry behind her, heard them splashing closer—but she didn't wait.

She didn't even attack the scorpions on the nearest stingray. Instead, she leaped farther into the scorpion armada. She landed on a stingray's back between three scorpions, and they struck at her—but they were slow and uneasy on the rippling tide. She ducked and spun and kicked them into the waves.

The three scorpions sank without a trace, and a pincer from a nearby stingray slashed at her.

With another howl, Orani backflipped off the stingray. A stinger missed her cheek by a toe pad's width just as she dove into the water. From beneath, the sky was blotted out by endless stingray bellies. She swam underwater, the sound of battle muffled, then grabbed the side of a stingray and pulled herself to the surface.

The scorpions shouted in fear at the sight of her. She dodged and punched and dove and swam and struck again.

Once she cleared that stingray of scorps, she bellowed, "Fire!"

On the beach, the catapults clattered and swung, lofting clumps of burning moss and gourds of pepper-bush goop at the seaborne scorpions. Flames blazed in the sky, sparks glimmered, and ash dusted the surf.

Scorpions screamed and splashed, then fell silent.

But another sound rose—a faint buzzing that grew steadily louder. Then the blue-banded bees hit, darting close and stinging hard.

Orani battled for what felt like hours, but the scorpions kept coming, and the bees kept stinging, until she and her squad were driven back to the beach. She stood dripping on the damp sand, caught a stinger in one hand and punched with the other, then yelled, "Don't slow down! Keep firing!"

"We're out of ammo!" a frog shouted from the catapults, slapping a bee from the air.

With a growl, Orani kicked a scorpion into the surf. "You know what to do!"

A team of bullfrogs toppled the catapults, forming them into a barrier—then they set fire to the sea grass.

"This won't hold 'em for long," the scout told Orani.

She rubbed her face. "We've lost the beach. We're trapped."

After the silence of the water, the clamor of battle struck Pippi like a fist. She closed her ears to the screams and made her way through mobs of rushing frogs—soldiers, medics, hoppers—to the square outside the town hall, which Old Jir had turned into a command post.

"We need the Kulipari!" Arabanoo was saying when she waddled up. "We needed them hours ago."

"I'm holding them in reserve," Old Jir told him, looking even paler than usual. "You know the Kulipari."

"I do." Darel's mother looked up from the puff-ball bombs she was assembling. "Once they start using their poison, they won't stop until they're completely tapped out."

"Exactly." Jir rubbed his face. "If they start too early, they'll run dry before we even set eyes on Marmoo."

"Where *is* Marmoo?" Arabanoo asked.

"Out there somewhere." Old Jir's nostrils flared. "Waiting."

Pippi gulped in fear and her eyes slid toward the sound of the scorpion army crashing through the woods. Smoke from distant fires drifted over the village, past the streaks of silken thread that glimmered in the air: floating strands of night-caster silk.

Pippi's bill curled downward: Anyone who touched that webbing fell limp to the ground. Not dead . . . until Marmoo's troops reached them, anyway. She swallowed the lump in her throat and looked toward the medical area, where Coorah's father and his apprentices were treating injured frogs and platypuses.

"So we'll wait, too," Old Jir continued. "Once everyone's gathered in the village, the Kulipari will tap their poison and protect our retreat."

"And the turtle troops will be waiting?" Arabanoo asked.

"That's the plan."

"Where *are* the turtles?"

"I don't know." Old Jir inflated his throat unhappily. "They should've been here this morning." He paused as threads of spider silk shimmered with golden light and burned to ash in the air. "At least we have Yabber and his apprentices."

"We've also still got frogs trapped in the banyan trees," Arabanoo said. "Surrounded on all sides. We can't wait any longer for the Ku—"

"They got out of the banyan trees," Pippi told him. "They're on their way here and— Oh! There they are now."

Old Jir and Arabanoo followed her gaze toward the inner defenses, an enormous barricade of logs and vines and stone. Wounded tree frogs limped through the open gate, dragging the dead behind them. When the crashing of the scorpion horde sounded louder, a squad of wood frogs slammed the gate shut.

"That's the last of them," Old Jir said.

Arabanoo nodded. "We're all here."

"Almost all," Pippi said, thinking about the frogs who'd already fallen in the invasion.

"Yes . . . almost all," Arabanoo agreed, flicking his inner eyelids gravely.

After a moment, Old Jir hopped to the top of a speaking stump and lifted his walking stick. Frogs who'd been worm farmers and nursery-pool teachers a month earlier gathered around him; they were now the weary, battered commanders of the army of frogs.

"We lost the north," Old Jir ribbited. "We expected that. We'll make a stand here, with the Kulipari."

"Finally," a commander grumbled.

"If the village falls, we'll retreat to the beach. The turtles can help us reach the Coves, and—"

"Forget the beach!" Princess Orani landed in front of Old Jir's stump. "Marmoo's taken the beach."

Shocked gasps sounded over the crashing approach of Marmoo's horde. The snapping of pincers crackled in the air, joined by the twang of a spider archer's bow. Somewhere nearby, a frogling wept.

"How?" Pippi asked. "How did he . . . Scorps hate water!"

"He's got stingrays," Orani growled. "A flotilla of stingrays, unloading scorps on the beach."

"On their backs?" Arabanoo gasped. "No way."

Orani nodded. "A dozen battalions landed—I almost wet my warts."

"You mean you jumped into the surf and pounded them like a maniac?" Arabanoo said.

Orani gave a low, croaking laugh. "For a while.

There are too many of them, and the blue-banded bees are giving them air support. We can't fight in the sea and air at the same time. My bullfrogs are slowing them down—but not for long."

"So we're surrounded," Old Jir said.

"And I checked the coast with a dreamcasting," Yabber's voice said. "The turtles aren't coming."

For a moment, Pippi thought he was casting his voice into the square from far away, but then she saw him and his three dreamcasters stepping from the gloom of the town hall.

"The stingrays turned the turtles back to the Coves," Yabber explained, his face creased with worry. "Marmoo threatened their pups. The turtle soldiers couldn't blame them for trying to protect their young."

"Shell-heads . . . ," Orani muttered.

"Maybe Darel found some allies," Pippi said in a small voice.

"He didn't," Yabber told her, lowering his neck mournfully. "I've been tracking him with my dream-casting. Last I saw, he was two days' journey away . . . and hadn't found help."

"You're a dreamcaster!" Arabanoo snapped.

"Do something! Stop the stingrays, stop the bees—do something!"

"They've been turning the nightcasters' webbing to ash all day," Old Jir told him. "Otherwise, we'd have been trapped in a blizzard of silk hours ago."

"Indeed." Yabber looked toward the crash of the scorpion army in the woods. "And we've been turning firm ground to swamp."

"That's what's slowing them down?" Arabanoo asked.

"They aren't good in quicksand," Yabber said with a glint of satisfaction in his eyes. "Plus, I've been leading Commander Pigo's squad in circles all day."

"We planned to retreat," Old Jir told his commanders, "but there will be no retreat. This is where we stand. This is where we fall." He raised his walking stick. "Move the river!"

22

T OLD JIR'S COMMAND, A SQUAD OF wood frogs strained at levers high atop the waterfall. With great effort, they were able to move them far enough to release heavy boulders into the river, which blocked the current. The water splashed into new channels freshly dug by the burrowing frogs. The old river ran dry and dozens of new streams started to fill, spreading across the village like miniature moats. Pond frogs grabbed spears and hooks and leaped into the channels, swimming for fortifications.

Pippi looked anxiously toward the barricades. Through the cracks between the logs, she saw spider archers climbing the wall, and heard their shrill screams when frog defenders knocked them off. She moved to join them, then stopped when the crowd gasped.

The scorpion horde had reached the village. But that wasn't the only reason why the crowd had gasped.

The Kulipari were on the roof of the town hall. Burnu stood in the center, his boomerangs in his hands, and Dingo crouched beside him, an arrow nocked. Quoba's cloak fluttered in the breeze as she raised her staff in a silent salute, then dropped from the roof.

"I thought the Kulipari were special," Burnu called to the watching frogs. "I thought we were better than ordinary frogs. But watching you today, I saw true heroes. Your courage rings out across the Amphibilands . . . across the entire outback." He inflated his throat as his gaze swept the frogs. "But now, my brothers and sisters, it is time to attack."

He raised one boomerang overhead, and the cry of "Kulipari!" resounded across the village.

Squads of burrowing frogs squirmed into tunnels, and wood frogs took cover behind camouflaging leaves. In the branches, tree frogs unraveled vine lassos, while pond frogs and platypuses held the other ends, ready to drag scorps into the water.

Amid the bustle, the deep croaking of alarmed bullfrogs sounded from the direction of the coast. Pippi shifted uneasily. Those were Orani's frogs, driven toward the village by Marmoo's seaborne

troops, which meant the enemy was only moments away from—

FWOOMP! The earth shook as one section of the barricades fell, and screams and shouts and panic filled the air.

Taking a quick breath, Pippi started forward to help the defense.

"Pippi!" Yabber said from inside the town hall's front doors. "Over here!"

She turned, and frog warriors leaped over her as she rushed to Yabber. "What? What should I—"

"Stay close," Yabber told her. "I might need—"

The bloodthirsty roar of the scorpions and spiders pouring through the gap in the barricades drowned out Yabber's voice. Pippi stared in horror as a wave of arachnids smashed into the frog defenders, snapping and stinging and shooting silk. Wood frogs leaped into battle from behind the leaves, ambushing a squad of scorpions and driving them into a watery channel that ran alongside the fallen barricade.

The panicked scorpions clawed for dry ground— but their fellow scorpions trampled them underwater. The arachnid army kept pushing forward, shoving the scorps in front toward the village, filling the defensive trenches with carapaces.

The scorpions slammed into the final remaining squad of wood frogs holding the gap between the barricades. Arabanoo landed beside the squad, hacking at the scorpions with a hatchet in each hand. Spider archers shot webs at him from the top of the barricade, and he dodged and shouted until Orani landed beside the spiders and bellowed, "You mess with the bullfrog, you get the horns!"

Which didn't make sense, but Pippi wasn't about to complain.

Orani lashed the spider archers off the barricade, using a tree vine as a whip, and the wood frog squad roared. Arabanoo led the counterattack . . . but nothing could stop Marmoo's horde for long.

Until a glowing blur zigzagged through the writhing black mass of scorps, and segmented stingers collapsed like reeds before a scythe. Quoba leaped over a scorp, flashing through the gap in the barricades to the outside, her staff spinning faster than Pippi's eye could follow. She kicked another scorp into troops of spider archers, then appeared on the other side of the battlefield, surrounded by the enemy. They slashed at her, then fell with short screams as she cut them down.

From the front doors of the town hall, Pippi peered

through the gap. Quoba seemed to be everywhere at once—and soon the scorpions realized there was an enemy in their midst. They stopped advancing on the barricades, and turned inward, surrounding Quoba.

"Yabber!" Quoba yelled. "Close it up!"

Pippi turned to Yabber. "What does she mean? Close—"

Yabber's eyes glowed golden, and vines started sprouting in the gap between the barricades, growing incredibly fast, rising to replace the log wall with living plants. The scorpions' pincers flashed, trying to cut the tendrils, but Quoba was suddenly among them, her staff cracking carapaces, while Burnu's boomerangs slammed into the spider archers atop the barricades, who were aiming at Quoba.

In a moment, the dreamcast vines filled the gap, repairing the barrier, shutting out the scorps on the other side . . . along with Quoba.

"Yabber!" Pippi gasped. "Quoba's stuck outside with the scorps."

"The scorps," he said, his voice hard, "are stuck outside with Quoba."

"Up there!" Orani yelled, pointing skyward. "Flying scorps!"

Pippi raised her head and saw Commander Pigo

and his elite troop drifting into view above the now empty nursery pond, dangling from long tendrils of glowing spider silk.

"They're ballooning in!" Old Jir shouted. "Dingo!"

Before he finished calling Dingo's name, dozens of arrows blackened the air from the roof of the town hall. Half the scorpions thudded to the ground inside the fortifications, but the other half sliced the spider-silk tendrils with their own pincers. A dozen red-banded scorps thumped to the ground and scuttled to sting the frog defenders from behind.

Arrows stuck out of the scorps' carapaces like an echidna's spines—then Burnu struck like an avalanche, his eyes black and his skin glowing. He crushed scorpions with spinning kicks and slashed his boomerangs like claws. Pippi gulped as Burnu wailed a terrifying war chant, tearing through scorpions in a brutal frenzy.

Web-nets twirled through the air toward Burnu. Elite spider archers loosed volley after volley. Burnu dodged easily, but the webbing caught dozens of other frogs and dragged them closer to the spider soldiers . . . until Dingo's arrows pierced them.

Burnu leaped to free the frogs, and another squad of red-bands faced him, along with the scorpion Pippi recognized as Commander Pigo. Dingo must've recognized him as well, because a volley of arrows flashed at him.

Pigo deflected them with a blur of flashing pincers. "You can't beat us all," he grunted to Burnu. "You'll run out of poison before King Marmoo runs out of soldiers."

"We'll last long enough to beat *you*."

With a gesture of his tail, Pigo ordered his scorpions to scuttle closer, surrounding Burnu. "You can't stop us. Maybe if you surrender, King Marmoo will . . ."

Burnu cracked his neck. "Will what?"

"Kill you quickly," Pigo told him.

Orani jumped onto a red-banded scorpion warrior nearby, flattening him into a tangle of legs and pincers.

"Maybe we can't *stop* you," Orani said, laughing. "But we can *stomp* you."

Burnu laughed along. "There's your answer, scorpling," he told Pigo, and glowed even brighter.

He launched himself at the scorpion commander, hurling his boomerangs, and the two of them traded vicious blows, faster than Pippi could follow. They separated, both bloodied, and a boomerang slammed into Pigo's knee. Burnu leaped forward, grabbed hold of Pigo with his toe pads, swung him in a tight circle, and drove his elbow into the scorp's carapace.

A sharp *crack* sounded, and Pigo roared with pain. Then a blizzard of leathery wings swept across the battleground and turned the whole world white. Ghost bats swooped at Yabber, who was standing on the front step of the town hall, their red eyes gleaming and their needle fangs flashing.

Pippi shouted, "That's *my* turtle!" She did a half-handstand and lashed out with her spur.

She missed, and a ghost bat bit her leg. She squealed and slapped the bat to the ground with an angry thwap of her tail, then smacked it again and again as a brisk wind swept past her.

Not just brisk: powerful. And not just a wind: a tornado.

The ghost bats hissed and flapped and tumbled through the air, shoved by a golden glow shining from inside the town hall, behind Pippi.

"You heard the platypus," Yabber said, his eyes as bright as the sun. "That's *her* turtle."

She shut her eyes against the dreamcast windstorm and almost laughed. Then she heard the *FWOOMP! FWOOMP! FWOOMP!* of more barricades falling.

The laughter died in her throat. She closed her ears and nose, and "listened" with her bill. She felt the tingle of the battle tumbling closer as the scorpions rampaged through the barriers and smashed into the frog defenders. She felt scorpions splash into the watery trenches, shoved forward by the battalions still marching toward the village. Soon the channels were crammed with scorpions, and the next waves of the arachnid army simply advanced over their fallen comrades.

Pippi trembled and opened her eyes. Dust from Yabber's windstorm and floating debris from the fallen barriers still filled the village. With a sick dread in her stomach, Pippi looked around for the reassuring glow of the Kulipari.

Instead, she saw a black shape flash through the dust, bigger than any normal scorpion. *Marmoo*. And spider nightcasters clustered behind him, unspooling silk into the air.

All of the barriers had fallen, all the watery channels were crammed with scorpions. The ghost bats circled the village, driving stray frogs toward the town hall and snacking on bees when they thought the scorps weren't looking. Orani and her bullfrogs faced the arachnid legion that had arrived on the stingrays, while Burnu stood with the tattered frogs at the shattered barriers.

Strands of nightcast silk slithered through the air toward the town hall, then glimmered with golden fire, flared with flames, and vanished. Ash drifted lower and dusted Arabanoo, who was sprawled motionless on the ground with a stinger wound in his shoulder, Gee's mother standing guard over him.

A surge of grief rose in Pippi's heart. "No," she whispered, fearing the worst.

Then Gee's mom lifted Arabanoo and hopped toward the medical area, and Pippi saw that he was still alive.

"Thank the stars," she murmured, exhaling deeply.

Her relief died a moment later, when Marmoo leaped into the center of the now destroyed marketplace. He loomed over Pigo, and his carapace glimmered with strange, unsettling grooves.

"Darel!" he growled. "I want the frog called Darel!"

23

INGO LEAPED THROUGH THE AIR AND landed on her hands on the speaking stump.

"I'm sorry," she told Marmoo, flip-ping onto her feet. "Darel's not in right now. Can I take a message?"

"Don't mock me, croaker!" Marmoo snarled.

"Why not?" she asked, scratching her head. "What're you going to do? Get *more* evil?"

Marmoo slashed his tail at Dingo, and when she leaped away, his stinger stabbed the stump, which he then tore from the earth, roots and all, and hurled into the market stalls.

Pippi whimpered. Maybe Pigo was right. Maybe nothing could stop him.

"Bring me that wood frog!" Marmoo roared, scraping a groove in the stones underfoot with one pincer.

Quoba stood facing Marmoo, though Pippi was *sure* she hadn't been there a moment earlier. In fact, the last she'd seen, Quoba had been trapped outside the barricades with the scorpions.

"No," Quoba said.

Burnu strolled up beside Quoba, holding his boomerangs absentmindedly, like he wasn't even scared. "Yeah. What are we, wood frog delivery?"

"The Veil is down." Marmoo's segmented tail curved and swayed. "The Amphibilands are mine. There is no way to stop my horde now."

"We could arm-wrestle?" Dingo said from the town hall steps. "Or play rock-paper-scissorfish?"

"If you could defeat me," Marmoo said with a hungry smile, "my horde would walk away. But you cannot."

Old Jir stepped around the stump that shattered the market stalls. "Before you were a scorpling, Marmoo, the golden frog defeated a horde like this."

Marmoo snorted. "The golden frog is a myth," he said, jabbing his stinger into a thick root. "A boogeyman we scorpions use to scare our children."

"He was as real as you or me." Old Jir glanced aside briefly, and for a second Pippi wondered what he was looking at. "And he believed in preparation."

"He can't help you now." Marmoo lifted a length of dirt-clumped root with his stinger. "Nothing can."

"Perhaps not, but—"

Marmoo hurled the root at Old Jir. A stocky wood frog leaped to block the root, but it spun wildly and struck Old Jir a glancing blow in the chest. He fell and wheezed, and the frightened gasps of frogs sounded from all around.

Marmoo didn't seem to notice. His scarred side eyes scanned the battlefield. "Commandeer Pigo! Report!"

Pigo stepped into sight with a shatter mark on his carapace from his fight with Burnu, and his tail broken near the stinger.

"My king," he said as he limped toward Marmoo with his sole surviving red-banded soldier. "The mission is complete. We drove all the frogs here, and the Kulipari are yours."

Marmoo sneered. "All the frogs except the one I want most."

"Darel isn't in the Amphibilands," Pigo said. "He left the—"

Marmoo smacked Pigo with his pincer. "You're a disgrace! Look at you! Half broken, weak as a softskin!"

Pippi looked away from the scorp squabble—in the direction that Old Jir had glanced. From her spot just inside the town hall, she saw Dingo stealthily pulling onyx-tipped arrows from a quiver strapped to her leg. Meanwhile, Quoba was standing in plain sight for once . . . but something about her face made Pippi think she was about to tap her poison. Or was checking if she still had any poison left.

"Maybe that's what Old Jir meant by 'preparation,'" she said to herself.

"Pippi," Yabber whispered, unfurling his neck until his mouth was beside her ear. "Listen for the Serpent."

"What?" she whispered back. "*Now*? Look at the Kulipari, they're about to—"

"I know!" he said. "But I'm fresh out of ideas. We need the Serpent. Can you hear anything? Is it watching? What next? What now?"

"I don't know!" Pippi couldn't hear the Rainbow Serpent—she couldn't hear anything except the moans of the injured and the hammering of her own heart. "I don't know!"

"Look at you!" Marmoo bellowed at Pigo, hitting him again. "You're no scorpion."

"I'm sorry, my—" Pigo started.

Marmoo slammed him to the ground. "'Sorry'? Sorry doesn't—"

"Eat toe pad, scorpion slime!" Princess Orani bellowed, charging forward.

"No!" Burnu blurted. "Wait—"

Too late. Orani slammed into Marmoo with her shoulder, and the impact thudded across the village. Marmoo slid a few inches and looked almost impressed. But not hurt. He cocked his head and said, "What are you?"

She punched him with fast blows. "I am Princess Orani, of the—"

"Of the defeated croakers," Marmoo snarled, and jabbed her with his stinger, flinging her across the battlefield.

She rolled limply to a halt at Burnu's feet, an ugly slash on her shoulder.

Burnu crouched and whispered a few gentle words while Orani moaned. And then his skin glowed so brightly that Pippi couldn't look directly at him.

"Kill him!" Burnu shouted and sprang forward in a streak of color.

In a black whirl, Marmoo spun to face Burnu, whose body arched in the air, coiled to strike. Five onyx-tipped arrows pierced Marmoo's shoulder and he roared—then Quoba's staff smashed into Marmoo's rear legs, and Burnu struck, kicking Marmoo's plated neck as his boomerangs smashed the scorpion lord's face.

Marmoo staggered, roaring in pain and rage . . . but despite his injuries, his tail whipcracked at Quoba and his pincer slashed at Burnu.

Burnu leapfrogged the pincer . . . right into Marmoo's tail, which struck his chest so hard that Pippi heard ribs snap. Quoba dodged the scorpion lord's stinger, but his pincer sliced her staff in half and snapped at her neck.

Quoba slid on her knees beneath the scorpion lord, now holding two short fighting sticks instead of a staff. She tapped more poison and jammed the sticks into Marmoo's soft underbelly. Except Marmoo wasn't soft anymore, not anywhere, and her sticks only scratched his nightcast-hardened carapace.

Marmoo's roar turned into a laugh as the strange spiderweb pattern on his carapace glinted with a sickly green light. His wounds blazed with an unearthly glow, then disappeared as they magically healed.

"Well, that's not good," Dingo said, firing her last arrows and launching herself into the hand-to-hand fight.

Marmoo batted her away with a pincer, stomping

at Quoba with four of his legs as he yelled, "Fahlga, web those turtles, *now!*"

Across the smoking village, the spider night-casters opened a row of cages and cracked silken whips. Dozens of geckos burst out, bolting toward the town hall—then the spiders unspooled threads from their spinnerets. Their eyes turned black and the silken strands slithered through the air above the panicked geckos, snaking directly toward Pippi and the turtles in the town hall.

"Webs!" she gasped, pointing. "Watch out!"

The turtle apprentices murmured, and a golden cloud billowed around them, like a thousand fire-flies tumbling toward the terrified lizards.

"Stop casting! Don't hurt the geckos!" Yabber snapped. "They're prisoners!"

The golden cloud broke apart. Pippi's bill tingled with fear and Yabber yanked her behind the pro-tection of his shell. She fell onto her butt, and the nightcast silk wrapped around the turtle appren-tices, glimmering with a sickly green light.

Pippi clenched her jaw. She couldn't watch this—turtles being killed by spider magic. She shot from behind Yabber, grabbed a turtle's flipper, and started dragging him away from the webbing.

She took two steps before the gecko stampede struck, knocking her to the ground. She gasped for breath, and a strand of nightcast webbing slithered toward her. Closer and closer. Her eyes widened in terror—then she caught a glimpse of something outside the town hall, beyond the geckos. Beyond the spiders in the ruined village, beyond Marmoo and the Kulipari. Beyond the battlefield . . .

An instant before the nightcast webbing struck, Yabber leaped in front of Pippi. The glowing strands wrapped him instead of her, clinging to his shell and wrapping his long neck.

And that's when the frogs outside started shouting: "The Blue Sky King! The Blue Sky King!"

Pippi fearfully peered through the town hall doors, looking high in the cloudless sky. Four harrier hawks soared toward the Amphibilands, talons curled and wings wide. Four frogs rode hawk-back, diving toward the battlefield. Blue war paint streaked the face of the frog in front, and a familiar dagger glinted in his hand.

24

AREL LEANED OVER THE NECK OF HIS harrier hawk, swaying in time to the beating of her powerful wings.

At first, the view from the air had taken his breath away. He'd been awed by the harsh beauty of the outback and its sheer size. But after flying for hours, he'd spotted a smudge of smoke on the horizon, and heard Coorah gasp beside him.

The Amphibilands was burning.

Darel flicked away tears with his inner eyelids. *He'd done this.* It was his fault. He'd told them to lower the Veil, and now the eucalyptus forest was on fire. Was his mom okay? Were the triplets? Was brave, furry Pippi still alive? Had the Kulipari fallen? What about Arabanoo and Gee's brother, Miro? Old Jir?

"C'mon, c'mon," he said, squeezing tighter with his knees.

"Kee-ee-kee-kee!" his hawk told him, and flapped faster.

"Thanks," he said, slitting his nostrils against the wind.

As they swooped closer, Darel bulged his eyes at the sight of the Outback Hills. A writhing mass of scorpions skittered over the destroyed frog defenses, creeping past a thick pillar of smoke.

"The Baw Baw village," he gasped. "It's—it's gone."

A scar of toppled trees surrounded the great banyans, and spiders climbed through fallen branches, dangling from strands and spinning webs. The wetlands—where his mom sent him to catch dragon-flies—had been trampled into mud.

"Look at the coast!" Ponto shouted above the wind. "In the shallows."

"Is that . . . ," Coorah started. "What *is* that?"

Darel turned his head toward the beach. Scorpions and spiders drifted across the water, then marched over a field of charred sea grass and into the woods. He frowned at the sight of shapes in the shallows that looked almost like the shadows of huge birds.

"Stingrays," Ponto said. "Carrying Marmoo's troops."

Coorah groaned. "Across the water? No way . . ."

"What about the turtle soldiers?" Gee asked, his voice worried. "Do you see any turtles?"

Ponto scanned the coast. "No."

Darel squeezed his eyes closed and tried to imagine a rainbow. *Please. Please, tell me what to do! Tell me something, anything!* But all he heard was the rushing wind in his ears. No help from the Rainbow Serpent. No help from anyone.

When he opened his eyes, he saw that his home village—the leaf village, the central village—had been overrun by Marmoo's troops. The barricades had fallen, and Gee's neighborhood was in rubble. Spiders lurked among the ruins of Darel's house, ghost bats slashed at the frog army with needle fangs, and a massive scorpion stood in the razed marketplace.

"Marmoo," Darel breathed.

A faint glow shone from underneath the scorpion lord—Quoba's colors—while Dingo crouched atop a shattered cart and Burnu stood up from a heap of rubble nearby.

"Faster," Darel begged his hawk. "Please."

His hawk angled into a dive as Quoba rolled out from underneath Marmoo's churning legs. Darel flinched when Marmoo snapped at her with his pincer, but she dodged it, then rolled into a crouch beside Burnu.

Dingo landed in front of them, her bow in her hand . . . but her quiver empty. She grinned at Marmoo, like she wasn't standing in the middle of a battle-field, and he slashed at her with his tail. Her skin glowed brighter and her bow twirled and blocked Marmoo's stinger. One of the scorpion lord's hind legs slammed Burnu, then his pincer slashed at Dingo and—

A brilliant yellow light shone from beside Darel.

"Ponto!" Coorah yelled. "What are you doing? You can't—"

Darel raised a hand to shield his eyes from the glow, and caught a glimpse of Ponto sliding under his hawk, bracing his feet on her stomach, and pushing off. The hawk shot straight upward, and Ponto plummeted toward the ground in a blur.

"Go, go!" Darel urged. "Dive!"

Wind whipped past as his hawk let out a kee and plunged toward the battle.

Down below, Dingo staggered from the lash of Marmoo's tail, while Burnu and Quoba flanked the scorpion lord. Dingo still managed to grin, though, and crooked a finger at Marmoo. For a second, Darel didn't understand why Dingo was taunting Marmoo, or why Burnu and Quoba weren't attacking. Then he realized that they were working together, maneuvering Marmoo onto the exact spot where Ponto was about to strike.

The scorpion lord must've realized, too. He lifted his scarred face and looked directly at Ponto, who was seconds from impact, his glow trailing him like a meteor's tail.

Marmoo didn't dodge, though. He didn't move aside. He just barked a command, and his troops—the scorpions and spiders, the lizards and bees and bats—roared and charged the tattered remains of the frog army.

Darel heard the croaks above the rushing wind: "Blue Sky King, Blue Sky King!"

Free-falling in a blur of speed, Ponto shone blindingly bright as the ground approached. Yet Marmoo still didn't move. He simply hunched in his carapace, drew his pincers to his chest . . . and waited for Ponto to hit.

The shock wave almost knocked Darel from his hawk. A mushroom cloud of dust and debris rose over the village. Frog and scorpion soldiers hurtled across the battlefield like leaves in a windstorm.

The impact flung ghost bats past Darel, half of them stunned and dazed and the other half hissing in panic at the sight of the harrier hawks.

With a vicious *keeeeee!* Ponto's hawk slammed into a ghost bat at a steep dive, slamming it toward the ground.

"Help me!" the bat hissed, and a dozen other bats swarmed the hawk.

"Keek-eek!" the hawk cried, slashing with razor talons.

One bat shrieked and spiraled down, but the others snapped at the hawk with hungry fangs, using quick, darting motions to stay away from the killing beak.

A cloud of white bats surrounded the *kee*ing bird, then disappeared from view as Darel's hawk dived lower and leveled out close to the ground. The wreckage of the village blurred past, then Darel tapped the bird's head and she dipped her wings, slowing just enough for him to leap to the ground.

He rolled a few times, then stood facing the dust cloud that had swallowed the Kulipari and Marmoo. Coorah and Gee landed beside him, and he looked from one to the other. He felt like the Blue Sky King should know what to say at a time like this, something rousing or meaningful, but he didn't. He just felt grateful that his friends were standing beside him—like they always did.

"I don't know about you two," Gee said, "but I just rode a *hawk*."

Coorah pulled out her fighting stick as scorpions clattered toward them through the dust. "We'll take care of this, Darel. You make sure Marmoo's down."

"The two of you against dozens of them?"

"Five of us," Pirra said, leading two bedraggled platypuses closer.

"More like four," Gee told her. "I'm going with Darel."

"More like *ten*," a bullfrog said, hopping from the wreckage with a battered tree frog squad. "Those poor scorps don't stand a chance."

⋖ 25 ⋗

THE NIGHTCAST WEBBING GLOWED around Yabber, and the golden sheen of his eyes dimmed. He collapsed, his long neck flopping to the floor of the town hall.

"Hold on, Yabber!" Pippi said, slashing at the web with her spur. "Hold on, hold on—"

"Pippi, y-y-you must stay safe," Yabber whispered. "Find a pl-pl-place to hide and—"

A terrible *BOOM* sounded outside, and splinters stabbed Pippi's face. The town hall exploded and the roof collapsed. Pippi yelped in shock and fear, then cowered as a heavy branch careened from the roof, falling directly toward her. *Crack!* The branch hit Yabber's shell an inch from Pippi's bill. Debris rained around her, and she would've been pummeled to death if the branch hadn't formed a sort of tent over her.

She shivered and whimpered until the crashing stopped, then slumped in stunned despair. "Yabber?"

She touched the shell that formed half of her protective tent. "Yabber?"

He didn't answer, didn't move. She rapped on his shell, but he still didn't respond, so she shook her head back and forth, trying to sense him. For a second, she couldn't. Then her bill tingled faintly, and she almost wept in relief.

He was still alive . . . barely.

At least the webbing was gone. Whatever had boomed outside must've blown the spider night-casters away. Still, she needed to hide Yabber, and quick. If the scorpions found him like this, unable to defend himself . . .

She shuddered, unwilling to finish the thought.

The spider archers fired a barrage of webs, but Darel leaped over them and slashed the silk in half. One web-bolt thumped his shoulder, but he managed to keep his balance and slam down onto a hairy spider's back, then jump away into the blinding dust cloud.

Darel closed his inner eyelids. Harsh breathing, gritty scrapes, and sudden screams sounded around him. Stingers slashed suddenly through the dust, and fangs glinted. He dodged and leaped and struck, fighting to get closer to the spot where Ponto had struck Marmoo . . . until a strand of silk caught his arm and tugged him backward.

"*Gah!*" he croaked.

"Darel?" Gee yelled from somewhere in the dust cloud. "Croako!"

Darel slashed the strand of spider silk, but two more strands caught his leg and threw him off balance. "Polo!"

"Croako!" Gee yelled.

Darel slammed his toe pads down, anchoring him to the ground. "Polo!"

The strands tugged harder and harder, trying to drag him to the spider who'd thrown the webs—and Darel tugged back harder and harder, until he suddenly leaped *toward* his attacker. A pair of shocked spider eyes appeared in the dust a second before Darel lashed out with both feet. The spider hurtled off and Darel hit the ground on his butt.

Gee hopped beside him. "Not too shabby."

"I've got to work on my landing." A sharp edge blurred through the dust, and Darel shouted, "Down!"

Gee dropped, and a spider blade sliced the air where he'd been.

Darel leapfrogged Gee, cut the spider down, and then found himself in a blinding, dust-filled brawl against what must have been every spider in the outback. Surrounded by grunts and screams and webs and fangs and legs and legs and legs, he battled closer to where he'd last seen Marmoo . . . until a glowing web slapped his side and his legs went limp.

Oh, no. He fell to his knees, his nostrils slitting in fear.

An elegant spider nightcaster crawled toward him through the dust cloud, flanked by brawny guards. "Blue Sky King," she murmured. "Marmoo will reward me well for bringing you to him."

"Then he'll sting you," Darel said, trying to keep his voice steady. "Just like he stung Jarrah."

The lady raised her hand and webbing cocooned Darel. She smiled coldly—then a thud sounded, and one of her spider guards disappeared into the dust.

"What is the—" she started.

Another thud sounded, and Gee said, "And *stay* down!"

Darel felt a surge of hope. Ha! Gee to the rescue!

The spider lady fired a dozen strands of silk into the dust cloud. They writhed in the air, like they were searching for Gee. The strands suddenly went taut, trying to yank Gee closer, but he copied Darel's trick, and came shooting from the dust like a brown cannonball.

Gee slammed the spider lady to the ground and shouted, "Nobody move, or the arachnid gets it!"

"Web him," the spider lady gasped.

Silken strands wrapped Gee, who struggled and kicked . . . until the strands glowed green around him. Then he went limp, and his breathing grew shallow and weak.

"Wait!" The spider lady peered at Gee's wrist. "What is that?"

Gee's unsteady gaze shifted toward his silken bracelet. "A . . . gift."

"From who?"

"Friend of . . . mine." Gee gasped a breath. "A trapdoor spider."

Her lip curled. "I know them."

"Good friends . . . of yours?" Gee asked hopefully.

"Not friends at all, but I'm not Jarrah. I honor all the spider tribes." The spider lady gestured, and the webs fell away from Gee and Darel. "And that bracelet means you're a member of their tribe."

"So now I'm a . . . spider?" Gee grinned weakly.

"Hide under this cart. We won't harm you." The spider lady showed her fangs. "But if Marmoo asks, you never saw me."

"Marmoo's finished," Gee gasped. "Ponto fell on him like a . . . boulder."

"Nothing can crack Marmoo's carapace," the spider lady said grimly. "Not even that."

26

THE SPIDER LADY'S WORDS ECHOED IN Darel's mind as he crept through the settling dust.

"Hope she's wrong," he murmured, tightening his grip on his dagger.

When he'd met the Rainbow Serpent, bright colors had shimmered along his dagger's blade, and he hoped—he prayed—that it was the one thing that could stop Marmoo. That the Serpent had touched his dagger with enough magic to finish this.

If it wasn't, he didn't know what else to try.

He flicked his inner eyelids as the dust cleared. The sight of the wreckage sickened him. The marketplace was gone. The front wall of the fly shop—Darel's home—had buckled, and the smoldering roof sagged to the ground. The town hall was a tangle of debris, and the tree frogs' branches were shredded. Flames flickered everywhere, and black smoke blocked the sun, casting the Amphibilands into gloom.

Across the battlefield, squads of scorpions and spiders drove the surviving frogs toward the central pond, which was already crammed with tadpoles and wounded warriors. Darel looked toward the crater where Ponto had landed on Marmoo, and the cracked edges were barely visible inside the thick cloud of dust.

Darel took two hops, and a handful of scorps scuttled between him and the crater. The squad leader barked, "Take him down!"

"The blue-faced one?" another scorp said, his side eyes shifting uneasily.

"Chase him!" the leader barked. "Sting him!"

"You don't need to *chase* me," Darel snarled, and leaped at the leader.

The world became a blur of lashing stingers and snapping pincers as Darel dodged and jabbed. A gash of fire opened on his side, but he barely noticed. His dagger slashed and his feet kicked, and when he finally paused for breath, scorps lay on the ground around him.

But more came. Always more. Dozens more—too many—scuttling from around the dust cloud that concealed the crater. Then a wart-raising scream cut through the clamor—*"Aiiiiiiiiiii!"*—and a red-banded scorpion staggered from a burning market stall, broken and limp.

A second later, Coorah lunged into sight, smashed the red-band one last time, and leaped beside Darel.

Her eyes widened at the sight of him. "Whoa."

"What?"

"The blue clay on your face is cracked and smeared like—like war paint. You look feral. Wild. You look like a nightmare."

Darel touched his face. "Sorry."

"Don't be," Coorah told him with a sudden wild smile of her own. "You look like a *scorpion's* nightmare. And a frog's last hope. Although . . ." She eyed the oncoming horde. "I see you left a few for me."

"You take the hundred on the left." He pivoted onto one leg and smashed a smallish scorp. "I've got the hundred on the right."

She tossed powder from her pouch at an oncoming scorpion, who reeled and screamed. "Where's Marmoo?"

"In there, I hope," Darel said, nodding toward the crater.

"Blue Sky King!" Arabanoo yelled, flinging through the air from one of the broken branches.

"Arabanoo!" Darel almost laughed. "You're okay!"

"'Course I am." Arabanoo landed in a crouch, a bloody bandage wrapped around his shoulder, and smiled at Coorah. "How come *you* don't have a cool title like 'Blue Sky King'?"

Coorah grinned. "What do you suggest?"

"Green Leaf Lady."

"Hey, that's not too"—she flicked a scorpion with her tongue, then smashed it with her stick—"bad."

Arabanoo eyed Darel. "You're still a mud-belly, though."

"Sap-licker." Darel snorted. Then he looked at Arabanoo's bandage. "Are you really okay?"

"Nope," Arabanoo admitted. "I got stung by a scorp and had to sneak away from Coorah's dad." Three more wounded white-lipped tree frogs landed beside him. "Well, *we* had to sneak away."

"*What?*" Coorah glared at Arabanoo. "You hop back there this instant! Maybe the poison didn't get into your bloodstream yet, but—"

"I didn't know you cared so much," he interrupted with a mischievous grin.

"Well, I do," she told him, completely serious.

His grin faded. "This is where I belong, Coorah. On the front lines. With you." He looked at her for a long moment, then turned to Darel. "Just tell me what you need."

Darel wanted to yell at him to get back to the medical tent, but he knew Arabanoo wouldn't listen. He knew he would've done the same.

"I need to find Marmoo," Darel said.

"We've got your back," Arabanoo told him, flicking a blue-banded bee from the air.

Coorah looked resigned. "Warts and all."

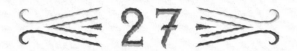

27

EBS ARCED ACROSS THE battlefield, and Darel shouted, "Jump!"

The frogs sprang apart. Arabanoo and Coorah headed for the spiders, while Darel leaped past a mass of scorpions. He gulped when a taipan snake slithered closer, and glanced to the sky, hoping the hawks might help.

Strands of webbing drifted above the treetops, and the hawks were gone. Probably driven away by the nightcast magic.

Darel adjusted his grip on his dagger and eyed the snake warily. Suddenly, a squad of burrowing frogs burst from the earth and struck at the snake with long hooks, dragging it underground.

"Thanks," Darel said, but they were already gone.

By the time he reached the crater, the dust cloud had settled. He hopped to the edge of the massive hole and almost landed on Dingo, who sprawled bleeding at his feet, her eyes half-closed and her legs twitching.

"Dingo!" he said, kneeling beside her.

"I'm out of poison," she gasped, her eyes closing fully. "We're *all* out of poison . . ."

A harsh crack sounded from the crater and Darel spun from Dingo and peered inside. Ponto lay unmoving in the bottom of the crater, and Burnu and Quoba looked barely able to stand, their colors faded and pale, as they faced Marmoo.

Two of the scorpion lord's legs dangled limply beneath him, and two more jutted out at sharp, painful-looking angles. But as Darel watched, the dangling legs shimmered faintly, growing visibly stronger, and the other two legs snapped back into place.

"If you tap your poison any longer," Marmoo crowed, "you'll kill yourselves and save me the trouble! But look at me. I'm only getting stronger."

Horror rose in Darel's stomach: Marmoo was right. Burnu and Quoba were about to burn themselves out, while Marmoo looked fiercer than ever.

Marmoo slashed Burnu with a pincer, then whip-cracked Quoba with his tail. He cornered them against the crater wall and pounded them over and over until neither moved. He lifted his stinger and—

"No!" Darel shouted.

In a flash, Marmoo leaped out of the crater and stood over Darel. "You," he growled, his ruined face triumphant. "*You're* the one I want."

Marmoo's stinger jabbed at Darel, and he desperately parried with his dagger—but the scorpion lord was too strong. The dagger was flung from Darel's grip and clattered to the cobblestones beside the smoldering ruins of a home.

Terror rose in Darel's chest: *Not my dagger! Not my father's dagger. Not my only hope! Not that!*

Marmoo's pincer closed around Darel's throat. "Do you know what I want with you?"

"I could—" Darel swallowed his fear. "I could probably guess."

"I don't want to kill you," Marmoo said with a mean smile. "At least not quickly. First, I want to thank you." He released Darel and gestured. "For all this. You lowered the Veil?"

Darel nodded, keeping his eyes on Marmoo's scarred face instead of looking toward the place where his dagger had landed.

"You handed me the Amphibilands on a platter," Marmoo said.

Darel braced his toe pads against the rubbled

earth. Marmoo was right; he'd done exactly that. But this wasn't over yet.

"All your water, all your land. The worm farms, the snail fields, the flies and bugs and beetles. Your homes." Marmoo inhaled sharply. "Even the air smells wet. So much water, and I will control every drop. Enough to rule the outback forev—"

Darel vaulted backward. He flipped in the air, landed in a crouch, and lunged for his dagger as scorpion feet charged toward him.

His finger pads closed on the dagger's hilt, but he didn't move. *Not yet, not yet.* Marmoo's tail lashed the air and Darel's heart clenched in his chest as he waited . . . then leaped directly toward Marmoo, low and fast, skimming just above the ground.

Perfect aim! He shot between Marmoo's legs, directly beneath his underbelly, and with all his might jammed his blade upward. Colors flickered, and Darel almost wept in relief: It was working!

Except the colors weren't from the Rainbow Serpent. They were sparks from his dagger scraping along Marmoo's carapace . . . but not stabbing through. His dagger—this last hope—hadn't been enough.

A biting pain flared in Darel's leg, and he found himself tossed into the air by Marmoo's pincer. For

a moment, it was as if time stood still. Tumbling high above the battleground, he saw the defeated Kulipari, the destroyed town hall. He saw his mother hugging the triplets in the central pond and a weakened Gee fending off a scorpion from under a cart. He saw dozens of spiders surrounding Coorah, who was kneeling beside the still form of Arabanoo.

All the violence made Darel sick. All the fighting, all the anger. All the bloodshed.

Then he fell, directly toward Marmoo's stinger . . . but Marmoo whipped his tail away at the last instant, and Darel slammed to the ground.

"I won't finish you that easily," Marmoo snapped.

Pain flared in Darel's leg, but he managed to stand. And with the images of wreckage and violence still flickering in his mind, he knew what he needed to do. He finally knew.

He jammed his dagger into his belt. "I surrender."

"What's that?" Marmoo barked at him.

"I surrender," he said louder.

"Shout it out, frogling!"

"We surrender!" Darel shouted. "The frogs surrender!"

Cries of surprise and dismay sounded from the frog army.

"I thought we could stop the bloodshed by shedding more blood!" Darel croaked. "But that can't work. That can *never* work. We have to surrender!"

Slowly, haltingly, the fighting quieted as the frogs laid down their weapons.

"We surrender!" Darel took a shaky breath and turned to Marmoo. "The Amphibilands is yours."

"It already was." Marmoo touched his stinger to Darel's throat. "It's mine because I took it. Do you expect mercy?"

Darel lowered his head to hide the fear in his eyes. "Sting me if you want. But let the others live."

Marmoo's tail whipped at Darel, clubbing him to the ground.

"Oh, I don't think so," Marmoo said, kicking Darel. "You'll suffer like we suffered. All who opposed me! Not just frogs! Not just turtles! Everyone who followed the Rainbow Serpent instead of the scorpion king!"

"Help him!" someone shouted. "Help the Blue Sky—"

"No!" Darel called. "No more fighting!"

"We'll march on the possums when we're done here!" Marmoo kicked Darel again and again. "The birds of prey and wallabies and every lizard tribe who didn't obey me! Trapdoor spiders, swamp crayfish, burrowing cockroaches—"

Darel curled into a ball as Marmoo ranted, taking the blows without fighting back, trying not to cry, trying not to moan.

Finally, Marmoo stopped. He raised his pincers and bellowed, "Everyone weak will suffer, everyone unworthy. The sun will burn you, the sand will whip you to tatters! Round them up, every last weakling, and drive them into the wastelands."

28

O N THE FAR SIDE OF THE BILLABONG, two legions of scorpions flanked a path of destruction where the underbrush had been trampled flat. They threw rocks and insults at the defeated frog nation, who walked between them.

Behind Darel, the weeping of frogs and the peeping cries of tadpoles mixed with the moans of the wounded carried on makeshift leaf stretchers. Darel's little sister didn't make a sound in his arms, though he felt her crying silently as he stroked her head. The other two triplets rode on Pirra's tail, while Darel's mom— injured in the fighting—limped alongside, leaning on a crutch.

Gee held Miro's hand and pretended he didn't see the tears streaking his brother's face.

Coorah followed behind, hopping among the stretchers. Darel hadn't seen a single tear from her, but her voice had been hollow with grief when she'd told him the news.

"Arabanoo took a stinger for me," she'd said. "He . . . he didn't make it."

Now she was treating the wounded with her father as the frog refugees trudged from the Amphibilands. Into exile. Into the certain death of the outback, jeered by scorpions and spiders.

Darel kept his head down, ignoring the pain in his leg that burned with every step. He didn't know if the other frogs blamed him for all the death, all the destruction. He didn't know if they hated him for lost family, for lost friends—for throwing away the only home they'd ever known.

He blamed himself, though. He hated himself.

After the scorpion jeers faded in the distance, Darel lost himself in a haze of pain and self-pity, sweating from the effort of pulling Dingo's stretcher. She still hadn't woken up. Neither had Ponto or Orani, who lay feverish and murmuring on their stretchers. Burnu and Quoba limped behind the other Kulipari, silent and faded and hunched over. They looked bad. Worse than Darel had ever seen. Because Marmoo hadn't simply beaten them—he'd stung them, and his poison still burned in their veins.

After endless hours, Old Jir put a hand on Darel's shoulder and said, "You did your best. We all did."

Darel just kept hopping, his eyes on the ground. He didn't want anyone to see his face.

Smoke clotted the morning air over the river and ash filled Pippi's nostrils every time she surfaced. At least the smoke hid her from the scorps grunting and feeding on the riverbanks.

After dragging Yabber from the wreckage of the town hall, she'd managed to shove him into a muddy channel without being spotted. Well, she'd managed to *roll* him into a muddy channel. But even that hadn't awakened him.

Pulling him through the water to the platypus burrows took hours of exhausting, terrifying work. Yabber's long neck flopped his head underwater if she didn't keep her bill high, and scorpion patrols crashed through the bushes while spiders climbed in the trees.

As night fell, Pippi finally reached the burrows— but she kept swimming under the full moon until she shoved Yabber onto the damp bank beneath the Stargazer burrow that Pirra and her friends had dug. The burrow mouth was too small for Yabber, so Pippi spent the rest of the night widening it, while keeping her ears cocked for any of Marmoo's troops. Finally, she shoved Yabber through, his shell scraping grooves in the burrow wall.

Then Pippi built a mud wall to hide them, added a few airholes, and collapsed into an exhausted sleep.

When she awoke in the morning and called out Yabber's name, he opened one eye and murmured, "Platypuses, I mean to say! Hidden depths," before falling back into an uneasy sleep.

Pippi wasn't sure how to heal a nightcast-sick turtle, but she figured that bringing him food was a good first step. So she swam in the smoke-shrouded river and swiveled her bill in the silt—until a powerful current slammed against her.

The water crashed and curled, sending Pippi tumbling bill over knuckles, churning through the river. When she shot to the surface in a panic, a tree splashed into the river just ahead of her. The wave washed her backward and another tree fell, and an-other, as the *thunk* of scorpion pincers sounded in the woods nearby.

Her heart pounding, Pippi swam desperately away, ducking branches as trees splashed all around her. Finally, she scrambled behind the curtain of vines at the burrow, and watched in horror as the scorpions chopped down the forest.

The day darkened as Darel led the frog refugees into the hills, past spindly shrubs and parched weeds. Weeping softened to whimpers, then to silence.

Finally, Darel told Gee, "That's far enough. Let's make camp."

"Yeah, Marmoo probably won't send his scorps after us now."

Darel looked at the wounded frogs behind them. "A few more days of this, and we might wish he had."

"Effie will help us," Gee assured him for the tenth time. "They've got a little water—and a lot of shade."

"Not enough," Darel said. But where else could they turn for help?

He didn't sleep that night. Instead, he moved from stretcher to stretcher, checking bandages and cleaning cuts. He rocked tadpoles to sleep in sloshing bassinets. The unsettling quiet of the outback spread across the camp as the moon rose and fell. And then, when dawn spilled over the distant mountains, he looked up from the splints he was making and spotted a scorpion stinger swaying above a nearby rise.

He almost shouted a warning—but stopped himself. He'd already surrendered. He'd already lost. The fight was over.

After taking a steadying breath, he crossed quietly to the rise. On the hillside below him, squads of scorpions skittered toward him, trailed by dozens of spiders. Except, on second glance, they were mostly limping, lurching, and stumbling. Every single one of them wounded.

Commander Pigo marched in front of the column, his carapace cracked and his stinger bent. He raised a pincer when he saw Darel. "Blue Sky King," he said in greeting.

"I'm just Darel, Commander Pigo," Darel told him.

"Are you?" The scorpion's side eyes shifted. "In that case, I'm just Pigo."

"What do you want?"

Before Pigo answered, a crowd of geckos rushed forward, zipping between all the scorpions' legs, toward Darel. "You're the frog!" one said in a crackly voice. "The flying frog!"

"I'm not—"

"Did you really visit our village?"

Darel nodded. "We wanted to—"

"Lots of us are hurt!" the gecko said. "Will you help?"

"If we can." Darel pointed toward Coorah's dad. "Bring your wounded to him and—"

"Thank you!" the gecko crackled.

Another gecko told Pigo, as she ran past, "Thank you, too!"

"The broken-tailed scorpion saved us from Marmoo!" a wounded gecko said.

Darel inflated his throat in surprise. "He did?"

"Marmoo wanted to eat us!" the wounded gecko said, limping toward the frog healers.

"You saved them?" Darel asked Pigo.

"Not exactly—"

"He did too!" another gecko said.

"I told Marmoo that eating the geckos was kinder than driving them into the wastelands." Pigo's mouthparts lifted in a twisted grin. "So he drove them into the wastelands."

"You tricked Marmoo?"

"There was a time," Pigo said, his grin fading, "when Marmoo was strong and clever and . . . a scorpion. But now? When the spider queen strengthened his carapace, she shattered his mind."

"He forced you out, too?"

Pigo nodded. "Marmoo said that getting wounded

proved that we're weak. So he gave every injured soldier a choice. Stay and be eaten, or leave forever."

"So you all left."

"Not all of us," Pigo said grimly. "Lady Fahlga disappeared, and others . . . stayed and paid the price."

For a moment, Darel didn't speak. He looked at Pigo, his sworn enemy, the scorpion who'd killed King Sergu. Sometimes, late at night, Darel still saw the old turtle king lying dead at his feet. But now he saw the cracks in Pigo's carapace and the pain in his eyes every time his broken tail swayed.

"Come on," he said with a sigh. "Let's see if frog medicine works on scorpions."

Pigo's mid-legs shifted in surprise. "I can't—I can't ask you to help us."

"You didn't ask," Darel told him. "I'm offering."

"Why? We're your enemy."

"You *were* our enemy," Darel said carefully. "Are you still?"

Pigo's side eyes shifted toward the spiders and scorps behind him. For a moment, he didn't answer, and Darel realized that Pigo was taking the question seriously—and that he'd answer honestly.

"No," Pigo finally told him. "But we're scorpions without a lord, and scorpions *need* a lord. We're broken and battered and maybe weak, but . . ."

Pigo and the other scorpions suddenly bent their mid-legs, and the spiders unfurled strands of silk.

". . . we pledge ourselves to you," Pigo continued. "To our new lord. To Darel, the Blue Sky King."

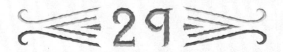

EE HOPPED TO THE EDGE OF THE ravine where the trapdoor spiders lived, and for the first time since leaving the Amphibilands, the weight of defeat was lifted briefly from his shoulders. Effie and her people would give the frogs shelter and water. He knew they would.

And not just the frogs. The platypuses and geckos . . . and *scorpions*. Gee bulged his eyes at the arachnoid form standing beside him. He couldn't get used to being this close to Pigo without fighting or fleeing.

But Pigo merely looked into the ravine. "He's very brave."

"Who?"

"The king."

Gee blinked at him. "Marmoo? Wait—you mean *Darel*?"

"I do," Pigo said with a nod. "After being enemies for so long, he invited us into his camp. That takes a rare kind of courage."

"Yeah, or he's a complete wart-head."

Pigo's side eyes glinted in what Gee thought was *probably* amusement. "Yes, or that."

Gee rubbed his face. When Darel had led the scorpions and spiders into camp that morning, froglings had wept and trembled, while older frogs murmured about revenge.

But Darel had jumped to the top of a heap of rocks and given a speech. "I don't know what the Rainbow Serpent wanted from us," he'd said. "I don't know what it *still* wants. But I know this—the Serpent is a spirit of rivers, not desert. Of life, not death. There can be no more fighting."

"So what do we do?" someone had called.

"We look for a new home."

"In the outback?" another frog had called. "In the heat and the sun and the dust?"

"There's no water!" a bullfrog had croaked from beside Princess Orani's stretcher.

"We'll die!" a tree frog had peeped.

"That's what Marmoo wants," a wood frog had said. "For us to die slowly."

"Keep the faith," Darel had told them. "We've lost too much to stop now."

Gee shook his head at the memory. "Well, you

know what Darel always says?" he asked Pigo. "His finest pearl of wisdom?"

Pigo turned to face Gee, his expression intent. "The king? No, please tell me. What is his wisdom?"

"He says, 'It takes all kinds.'"

"*That's* what the Blue Sky King says?" Pigo frowned. "That's his wisdom? That's like saying 'A bird in the pincer is worth two in the bush.'"

"I know!" Gee croaked with a snort. "That's what *I* told him! It's like 'Cleanliness is next to frogli—'" Movement caught his eye in the ravine. "What's that?"

Pigo shaded his main eyes. "Spiders."

"Marmoo's soldiers?" Gee asked, inflating his throat nervously.

"I don't know, I can't—"

A faint call sounded. "Look out, Gee! There's a scorpion *right there*!"

"Effie!" Gee shouted happily, and hopped into the ravine.

When Darel reached the bottom of the ravine, he found the spider mothers in a circle around Gee and Effie. "—so we need help," Gee was saying. "Food and water and a place to stay."

"Show them," one of the spider mothers told Effie.

Effie led Gee and Darel along the dry gully, and when they stepped around a craggy boulder, Darel gasped. The trapdoors were ripped open, exposing a dozen holes in the ground.

"Wh-wh-what happened?" Gee stammered.

"Scorpions," Effie said, her voice tight. "They came a little after you left. Marmoo doesn't just want the Amphibilands. He wants *all* the water."

Darel remembered the gecko water hole. "Did they steal yours?"

"They said our trickle wasn't worth taking. But they tore apart the trapdoors."

"Can't you rebuild them?" Gee asked.

Effie sighed. "Sure, but . . . Earlier this morning, the trickle ran dry."

Gee groaned and Darel swayed, suddenly light-headed, and reached for the craggy boulder to stay on his feet. He'd hoped the trapdoor spiders could shelter the refugees from the Amphibilands. But if they didn't have any water . . .

"Maybe Gee and I can find water," he said. "Frogs are good at that."

Effie led Darel and Gee into the underground spider village, to the massive cavern that Darel had seen on his last visit. The air still smelled damp and earthy, and Darel felt his parched skin absorb the moisture from the air, but when he hopped to the center of the room, the trickle of water was gone.

"Not a drop," Gee declared.

Darel looked toward the dark hole in the wall, into which the water had once flowed. He stepped closer and inhaled. "Smells wet, but . . . not watery. I wonder how far the tunnel goes."

"All the way," Effie told him.

"All the way where?"

She showed her fangs briefly. "I don't know! That's just what the mothers always say. And they don't know, either."

"What're we going to do?" Gee asked with a mournful ribbit.

"Keep moving," Darel told him, trying to sound more confident than he felt. "There's nothing else we can do. Except ask Effie's people to join us."

"You mean, leave here?" Effie asked, shifting uneasily.

He nodded. "You can't stay. If there's no water, there's no life."

30

URLED IN THE BURROW BESIDE A snoring Yabber, Pippi frowned at the last few larvae. Barely enough for one more meal. Well, at least sleeping and eating seemed to be healing Yabber. He'd opened his eyes a few times, and even smiled at her once.

Another few days, and maybe he'd wake up for real and—

Her breath caught. Something felt wrong. Something felt *missing*.

She shook her bill back and forth but didn't feel a tingle of approaching scorpions, so she waddled to the mouth of the burrow. She widened the airhole in the mud wall, and a strange scent reached her.

The river didn't smell like a river. It didn't *sound* like a river, either.

She opened the hole enough to stick her head out, and blinked in disbelief. The river was gone. The water was gone. All that remained was a mucky, waterless riverbed.

She stood there for a long time, then checked on Yabber. Still sleeping. She sneaked from the burrow and crept through the stumps of the riverside trees, following the destruction upstream. Without water, she and Yabber didn't stand a chance. She'd been fighting back tears for days, trying not to think about her family and friends, but seeing the Amphibilands' forests torn to shreds made her eyes feel swollen and hot.

She blinked a few times, then froze when she heard a scorpion voice in the distance. She couldn't make out the words, but the tone rang with command.

After a terrified moment, she exhaled. *Okay, Pippi. You can do this. You need to get closer. You need to find out what happened to all the water.*

She climbed through the dense underbrush until she reached a steep ridge. The voice sounded louder as she followed the ridge to its high point overlooking the central frog village. Her knuckles ached as she poked her bill through a leafy branch . . . Then her bill burned with a thousand tingles.

Scorpions packed the stump-covered hillside

beneath her, legions of them. One jointed tail swayed so close that she could've reached out and touched it. But none of the scorps saw her. They were all watching Marmoo pace in the valley where the ruins of the frog village still smoldered.

Every tree had been uprooted and dragged away: the paperbark tree overlooking the nursery pond, the entire tree frog village. Only the splintered remains of buildings were left.

"—led you to victory!" Marmoo was shouting as he stomped over the ruins of the marketplace. "The frog nation is broken, and all of this is ours!" He gestured with a pincer. "Water! Water is life. Water is power! But my scouts crept over every inch of our new land, and do you know what they found?"

"Didn't discover *me*," Pippi whispered.

"The water of the Amphibilands is connected to the springs and water holes of the outback! Our spoils of war, the prize for our victory, is being lapped up by the worthless and the weak all across the land!"

Scorpion soldiers muttered angrily and snapped their pincers.

"That's right!" Marmoo bellowed. "The frogs were stupid, as well as weak! They did nothing as their water trickled away into the outback—maybe they didn't even notice! But the age of the Amphibilands is over, and no water will escape the *Arachnilands*!"

The scorpions cheered.

"Enough!" Marmoo raised both pincers. "From this moment, nobody gets a drop of water—not unless they pay! Not unless they beg! Now the water is mine. The entire *outback* is mine!"

With three great leaps, Marmoo jumped from the valley onto the cliff where the waterfall used to spill from the rocks. He bellowed something Pippi didn't hear, to scorpions she didn't see, and a *creak-snap-thud* whip-cracked across the land, louder than a thunderclap.

Pippi's yelp of surprise was lost in the gasps and shouts of the scorpions.

When she peered toward the noise, she saw a huge wall of lashed-together tree trunks slam across the river that ran beside the marketplace. That's where all the trees had gone! The scorps had built huge walls with them. With the trees and the broken barricades, and even the walls of now destroyed homes.

The river current struck the wall—the *dam*, Pippi realized—and splashed and swirled and poured toward the village valley. *Creak-snap-thud!* Another dam slammed across the river on the far side of the village, and in the distance she heard the *thud, slam, splash* of dozens more.

Then with a roar that shook the earth, tidal waves crashed into the valley. Water churned the rubble with pounding tides, hungry waves swallowed the ruins, rushing currents flowed into the valley from every direction, clashing and spraying in white-water geysers . . . until, finally, everything grew still. Except for the cheering of scorpions and the pounding of Pippi's heart.

Marmoo must've been preparing this for days, Pippi thought. That's what had happened to the river outside the burrow. That's what had happened to every stream and creek in the Amphibilands. Marmoo had been moving them into position.

Now he controlled *all* the water of the outback. And water was life.

"Pippi?" Yabber said weakly when she returned to the burrow.

She rushed closer. "Right here! No, no! Don't go back to sleep until you have some larvae!" She fed Yabber a handful of larvae. "Much better! You look almost amphibian again."

"Reptilian," he murmured. "I'm a reptile."

"I know you're a reptile!" she said. "But you don't look *that* much better."

"You ridiculous marsupial—"

"I'm a mammal! A monotreme, as far as that goes, because laying eggs is the only smart way to have children, as if you didn't know. But that's not important. What's important is . . ."

She trailed off with a sigh. She needed to tell him about Marmoo's dam, about Marmoo hoarding the water. But before she gathered her thoughts, Yabber snored. He was sleeping again.

Pippi stroked his shell with fondness and fear. He was getting better, but he'd just eaten the last larvae— and without water, there was no food. Without water, there was no hope.

31

S DAREL LED THE MARCH ACROSS THE outback, he kept thinking about what he'd told Effie. *If there's no water, there's no life.*

The trapdoor spiders wove shady parasols—and slings and bandages and stretchers—but the sun still scorched delicate frogskin. No water, no life. Despite the tadpole bassinets being wrapped tightly, the water evaporated a little more every hour. Soon the bassinets would dry up completely—and tadpoles still needed water to breathe.

On the third day, a bullfrog tapped Darel on the shoulder. "The princess wants to talk to you."

Darel leaped up beside Orani's stretcher. "You're awake!" he said, relief washing over him at the sight of Orani sitting up. "How are you feeling?"

"I'm feeling ready," she said, struggling to her feet.

"Ready for what?"

"To strike back! We can sneak into the Amphibi-lands and attack. The scorps won't expect *that*."

"We lost, Orani," Darel said. "We already lost."

"Bullfrogs aren't made for all this wandering," she told him. "We stay in one place, we hunker down, and we never give up!"

She lifted one arm to rally her troops—then collapsed back onto the stretcher. Coorah was suddenly there, applying a poultice and scolding Orani for pushing herself too hard before she was fully healed.

Darel turned away, his shoulders slumped under the weight of responsibility. He didn't feel he'd "given up" when he'd surrendered, but maybe he had. Maybe he'd been wrong all along. He hopped toward his mother, to talk things through, but found her emptying her water gourd into a bassinet, with the triplets hunched beside her. His little siblings looked bad—tender frogling feet swollen, colors faded from the sun and dust—but they still smiled when they saw him.

"It's Darel!" Tharta announced to the tadpoles.

"Blue Sky Darel!" Tipi said.

"Tell us a story, D!" Thuma croaked.

He shook his head. "I don't know . . ."

"Go on, Darel," his mother said, her voice soft. "It'll take their minds off . . . things."

He couldn't say no to *that*, so he cleared his throat and began. "Well, once upon a time—"

"Tell us about the Snowy Mountains!" Tharta said.

Thuma jumped up and down. "The cave!"

"The *paintings*!" Tipi insisted.

"Once upon a time, I traveled deep into the heart of the Snowy Mountains," Darel told the tadpoles, "with the Kulipari and Yabber, the great turtle dreamcaster. And there we found a cave covered in drawings. Red and yellow outlines of rats and ostriches, snakes and wallabies. And spiders and scorpions and—"

"Frogs!" the triplets said all together. "And frogs!"

"That's right. But the most amazing part was a picture of the Rainbow Serpent stretching across the entire cave, over tunnels . . ." He paused as the memory flashed in his mind. "Tunnels and rivers and—"

"Tell us about the blob!" Tipi said.

"The blob!" Tharta said. "The blob!"

Darel lifted Tharta onto his shoulders. "Okay, okay! There was a picture of a huge flat blob."

"What kind of blob?" one of the tadpoles asked from a bassinet.

"I don't know. Quoba thought it looked like a

boulder, but Dingo said it looked like Ponto after he ate too much!"

A few of the tadpoles giggled.

"And beneath the blob," Darel continued, "there was a picture of a frog with a pointy tail. Except Burnu thought the frog looked like a cricket with pointy legs and—"

"We want to hear about the Tasmanian devils!" Thuma interrupted.

Darel talked and talked, trying to cheer up his siblings and the tadpoles. And he did, a little. But he kept thinking, *If there's no water, there's no life.*

They didn't need stories, they needed water.

Pippi followed the tunnels deeper into the burrow until she reached the dripping room. With the river gone, she'd been soaking a cloth with the condensation on the rock wall, then squeezing the water into a bowl.

She paused in the entrance of the dripping room and sighed. She'd lost track of the days since the Amphibilands fell. She'd lost track of her family and her friends. She slumped against the wall and stared at the water on the rock. Not trying to see patterns, not trying to decipher the Rainbow Serpent's messages.

Just thinking about her mom and dad and sister, and Gee and Coorah and Arabanoo, who'd saved the platypuses. About Chief Olba, who'd sacrificed herself. And the Kulipari, who risked everything in the fight against Marmoo.

And what about Darel? He was just a wood frog . . . just a kid, like her. But the Rainbow Serpent had given him the heaviest burden of all, telling him to tear down the Veil, to let Marmoo's hordes rampage across the Amphibilands.

And they had.

Pippi's eyes filled with tears when she realized how Darel must feel. Like he'd caused the death and heartbreak, like he'd helped Marmoo destroy his home and—

"Oh!" she blurted as a rainbow glinted on the dripping wall.

Then she snorted in embarrassment. That wasn't a rainbow, just the flicker of torchlight in her teary eyes.

Except . . . maybe she *did* see something. She peered closer, and the patterns looked like a dozen trickles flowing from a puddle to a boulder. Or like a dozen rivers flowing from the ocean to a mountain. But darker than normal rivers, or deeper . . .

⇒ 32 ⇐

THE DESERT HEAT SAPPED THE FROGS' strength. The geckos and spiders fared a little better, but soon Darel noticed that even the scorpions were flagging.

The last day of the journey before they reached the possum village was a blur of thirst and heat. Even the uninjured frogs stumbled every few hops and barely spoke. Darel knew they were conserving their strength for pulling stretchers and collecting dew for the tadpoles. The platypuses suffered even more, marching over the scalding, pebbled earth on tender knuckles.

That night, Darel dreamed of battle. Of Marmoo's gloating laughter and of the Amphibilands burning. Then the smoke changed to the darkness of a platypus burrow, and Darel found himself standing beside Pippi. She looked skinny and bedraggled, but he felt himself smile at the sight of her.

In the dream, she nudged him with her ridiculous bill. His smile widened. Pippi nudged him harder, turning him to look at a wet rock wall. Trickles of water slipped from a crack in the ceiling, spread across the wall, then joined together in a green puddle on the floor. Except the puddle was a pond, and the green was lily pads. Dozens of streams flowed across a great distance, then joined together in a—

"Ghost bats!" a spider scout shouted. "Stay low!"

Darel awoke with a start, his heart pounding and the dream fading. He scanned the sky and spotted motion near the yellow sunrise, bat wings flitting across the outback in the distance.

He watched until the bats disappeared over the horizon, then checked on the tadpoles and platypuses and geckos. He talked with Coorah and her dad, and spent a few minutes with the spider archers and Pigo's scorpions before giving the order to break camp.

A few hours later, Old Jir collapsed. Burnu and Quoba lifted him onto a stretcher the spiders wove, claiming they felt strong enough to handle the weight, even though Darel suspected they were tapping their poison when he wasn't looking. Ponto still hadn't awakened, but at least Dingo was on her feet again.

Then Coorah told Darel that the healers were out of medicine. "And we're running low on bandages, now that the spider mothers can't spin us new ones."

"Why can't they?"

"They're getting weaker," Coorah told him.

"No medicine, no water . . ." Darel looked toward the horizon. "At least we're almost to the possum village."

A soft hand touched his arm. "If we don't reach water today," his mother told him, "half of us won't see tomorrow."

"The possums will share," he promised her. "They don't have much, but they'll share."

"You'll see us through." His mom squeezed his arm. "I know you will."

But hours later, when they reached the outskirts of the possum village, Pigo skittered beside Darel. "My king," he said. "One of—"

"Would you stop calling me that?"

"One of my scouts spotted the ghost bats again," Pigo told Darel. "Flying toward the possums."

Darel looked toward the possum woods rising from the plain. "How many?"

"A legion."

"Too many to fight when we're this weak," Gee said, hopping in worry. "Maybe if they play dead, the bats will leave them alone."

"The bats eat dead things," Pigo said grimly.

"We need to *do* something." Gee gulped. "C'mon, Darel."

Darel blinked at him. "C'mon, what?"

"C'mon, c'mon!" Gee said, rubbing his hands together. "Think of something!"

"How am I supposed to think of anything when you're hopping around like a—" Darel stopped. "I just thought of something."

"That proves it," Gee said. "Hopping around works!"

"Follow me," Darel told Pigo, "but stay out of sight until I tell you."

Darel leaped through the scrub toward the possum village, hearing Pigo close behind him. The scuttle of scorpion feet still made him nervous, and he wanted to spin around to check that Pigo's stinger wasn't slashing at his back. But he looked to the sky instead, and saw ghost bats swarming toward the possums, from the west.

From the west. *Hmm.* Darel sped around the village to the east, then started racing closer.

When he spotted the slides and rope bridges of the village, he told Pigo, "Hide behind that rock. Don't come out until I raise my arm."

"What are you—"

"Just do it!" Darel snapped, then leaped forward and shouted, "Nioka! Possums! It's me—Darel!"

He landed high in a leafless bush, the thorny branch prickling his feet. He shouted again, and the possums gathered in the trees and leaf-strewn gardens, gazing toward him. Toward *him*, instead of toward the ghost bats, who approached from behind them in a silent deadly cloud.

"The frogs are back?" the possums said. "Maybe they'll know what to do!"

"Behold!" Darel shouted at them. "I am the Blue Sky King!"

"The what? The who?" they murmured. "What's he talking about?"

"My power has grown!" Darel bellowed. "And you have angered me!"

"We've *what*? That frog's spent too long in the sun . . ."

The ghost bats swooped toward the unsuspecting possums from behind, fangs bared.

"Now suffer my wrath!" Darel shouted, raising his arms. "And *die*!"

As he lifted his arms overhead, Darel heard Pigo step out from behind the rock. He was visible to the possums but not to the bats. Almost immediately, a tremor ran through the possums, and then every single one of them fell to the ground as if stone-dead, scared stiff by the sight of Pigo.

The ghost bats hissed in fear. *"What? No! What did the frog do?"*

"He killed them with his magic!"

"That's right!" Darel shouted at them, waving his arms. "And you're next!"

The bats spun in the air, flapping furiously away. *"Fly!"* one hissed. *"Flee! Reinforcements!"*

"Reinforcements, yes! Faster, faster—"

Darel ranted at them, shouting threats and waving his arms until they disappeared.

"Now *that*," Gee said, hopping closer, "was king-errific."

"Very clever," Pigo said, snapping a pincer in satisfaction. "Surely the possums will share water with us now."

But they didn't.

After they came to, they scolded Darel for terrifying them. Then while the possum healers scurried from stretcher to stretcher, holding pots of medicine with their tails and applying it with their hands, Nioka told Darel the bad news. "Our water hole is dry."

"What?" Darel said, a hollow pit forming in his stomach. "When?"

"Yesterday. It drained away."

"First the trapdoor spiders, now you?" Darel frowned. "It's like all the water is . . . connected."

"It's like all the water is *gone*," Gee grumbled.

"Something's happening," Darel said, slitting his nostrils thoughtfully.

"Water's running out," a possum said. "That's what's happening."

"Something big," Darel said, lost in thought. "Something *huge*. This isn't over. The Rainbow Serpent is still with us."

Effie nodded. "The mothers feel it, too."

"The Stargazer would know," Pirra said, tears in her eyes. "Pippi would know, if she wasn't . . ."

"She's alive," Old Jir said from his webbed stretcher, his voice certain even though he couldn't possibly know. "And Darel's right. The Serpent is with us."

"Where's it hiding, then?" Burnu grunted as he sat heavily on a tree root. "I don't see any rainbows."

"I don't know," Darel admitted.

The possums didn't have water, but they had edible flowers and juicy seedpods. They cooked a feast, and that evening the refugees from the Amphibilands ate a real meal for the first time in days.

Darel dug into a roast leaf sandwich and only halfway listened to the conversation.

"We're eating all your food," Gee said, his mouth full of pigweed. "Shouldn't we save some for you?"

"Nah," his burly possum friend told him. "None of this will last long in the outback heat."

"So keep it in your root cellars."

"We can't stay here without water." The possum grabbed a barbecued blossom with his tail. "We're leaving the village. We're leaving home. This is our last feast before we join your trek."

"Our trek? We don't have a trek! We don't know where we're going!"

"We might," Darel said.

33

DAREL HOPPED INTO THE DRY POSSUM water hole and turned to face the crowd.

"When the Rainbow Serpent told us to lower the Veil," he croaked, "we lost friends and family . . . and water. We wandered in the desert, asking for help. But the trapdoor spiders' underground river ran dry. And look at this." He stomped on the dry ground. "Another empty water hole." He paused. "How is this happening?"

"First Marmoo took the Amphibilands," Burnu said, chewing on a seedpod. "Now the water's drying up. He's doing it."

"That's true," Darel replied. "But this water hole's been getting lower for years. Before Marmoo. And the same is true of the trapdoor river."

"So the outback's been drying up for a long time?" Coorah asked.

"Maybe since King Sergu raised the Veil," Darel said. He ignored the murmur of shocked voices.

"Maybe that's why the Rainbow Serpent wanted us to lower it—to share water with the possums and spiders and everyone else."

"Except you're—" Pirra started.

"Not sharing with anyone!" a gecko crackled.

Pirra curled her bill. "Because Marmoo—"

"Took your water!"

"Yeah," Pirra said, "and now—"

"Things are even worse than before!"

"Stop interrupting," Pigo told the gecko, who flicked his tongue in fear and fell silent.

"Things *are* worse, though," Effie agreed. "We lost our home, too."

Pigo gestured around the dry water hole. "We need to—" Half of the possums fell to the ground at the sight of his pincer. "Sorry."

"What we need," Darel said, "is a new home."

"A new Amphibilands?" Gee asked.

"A new land for *everyone*," Darel said.

"But how?" a platypus asked. "Where?"

Silence fell. An expectant, hopeful silence, as everyone eyed Darel for the answers.

He inflated his throat, and looked from face to face to face. At least this time, he had a plan. "How is Marmoo drying up the possums' water hole," he asked, "when he's in the Amphibilands and we're out here?"

"Nightcasting!" someone yelled.

"No," Darel said. "I think it's because they're *connected.* The Amphibilands, the rivers, the water holes, the springs—they're all connected."

"How are they—" Gee started.

"Underground," Darel said. "The platypuses dug tunnels for the Rainbow Serpent. The trapdoor spiders did the same, and—"

"So did we!" a gecko crackled.

"And so did the geckos," Darel added, though he hadn't known that. "Tunnels crisscross the outback—underground rivers where water once flowed."

"But if they're dry," Coorah asked, "how does that help us now?"

"Because these tunnels will lead us to a green and watery land."

Cries of *Where?* and *How far?* came from the crowd.

"I don't know! All I know is this—" Darel crouched and drew two *X*s in the mud, an arm length apart. "This is the Amphibilands, full to the brim with water. And here's the trapdoor spider village." A few feet away, he drew another *X*. "This is where we are now. The geckos, your village is . . . where?"

A gecko ran up beside him and drew an *O*. "There!"

Darel straightened, then gestured to the *X–X–X–O*. "Look at that. Do you see what I see?"

"It's a line," Gee said, his eyes bulging. "It's a straight line."

"Leading from the water of the Amphibilands, straight across the outback."

"What kind of line?" Effie asked. "A line of what?"

"The Rainbow Serpent's tunnels are *rivers*," Darel said, smiling for the first time in days. "Showing the way. The way to water."

"But . . . how do we know they're leading *to* water, not just *from* water?"

"The Serpent told the platypuses, spiders, and geckos to dig these tunnels," Darel told her, still smiling. "And an ancient water spirit didn't build underground rivers to guide us into the desert. Rivers start in water, and they end in water, too. These tunnels will lead us to our new home."

Darel's smile didn't last long. As the refugees prepared to continue the march into the desert, Orani took him aside. "We're staying," she told him.

"You're what?"

She scratched at her bandage. "Staying in the possum village."

"There's no water here, Orani. The gardens will die; the trees will wither. You can't stay."

"We're bullfrogs. We don't crisscross the outback. We find one pond and we stick to it."

"But—" Darel gulped. "But I've finally figured out what the Serpent wants! We know where the water is now, right? In the Amphibilands. And we know that underground rivers connect it to . . ." He inflated his throat. "To *somewhere*. We just have to keep moving and we'll find our new home!"

"We're staying," Orani repeated stubbornly.

"You can't! This village is dying!"

"What if Marmoo comes after us?" she asked. "What then?"

Darel shook his head. "I . . . I don't know."

"We're not running anymore," she said. "Anyone who can't keep marching is welcome to join us, but we're done. The bullfrogs are making a stand. Right here."

Darel tried to change her mind, but she was as stubborn as she was strong, and she kept insisting that bullfrogs simply didn't wander across the desert. He knew what she was really doing, though: protecting

the refugees from being pursued. Sacrificing herself—
and her bullfrogs—to give him time to find this "new
home."

Pigo didn't pretend to understand amphibians and
marsupials and platypuses—whatever *they* were.
He'd pledged himself to the Blue Sky King because
he honored strength, and the wood frog was mighty.
Not in muscles but in heart. Still, the renewed hope in
their eyes when they left the possum village was more
than he could bear. So after saying good-bye to the
brave bullfrogs and marching all morning toward the
scorching dunes, he scuttled beside Darel.

"My king," he said with a little bow.

"You're never going to stop with that, are you?"
Darel asked, slitting his nose like a frog sometimes
did. Maybe in amusement.

Pigo gazed into the desert ahead but didn't say
anything.

"What?" Darel asked.

"We're heading straight in that direction?"

Darel nodded. "Until we hit water."

"Scorpions have ranged this desert for years.
There's no water there. There's nothing but the
killing sands."

"There has to be," Darel said.

Pigo fell silent. He didn't want to tell the Blue Sky King that he was wrong—dead wrong—but he was.

Then, to Pigo's shock, Darel put a soft frog hand on his shoulder. "I believe you, Pigo. I even trust you. But there's one thing you're forgetting."

"What's that, my king?"

"Two things," Darel said, his nostrils slitting again. "One, call me Darel."

"I'm sorry, my king," Pigo said, shifting his side eyes.

Darel smiled. "And two, Marmoo said that we're living in the new days of legend, right?"

Pigo nodded. "He did."

"In the new days of legend," Darel told him, "water flows in the killing sands."

At those words, Pigo felt a strange stirring in his thorax. Fear? No. Hunger? No.

Hope? Yes. Yes, he was feeling hope.

The feeling lasted for the rest of the day—and the next one, even as the Blue Sky King led his refugees into the bleak, barren dunes. Pigo's scorpions didn't mind the heat, even though they were pulling most of the stretchers, but his spiders started to sidle uncomfortably at the end of the second day.

That's when Pigo looked more closely at the other creatures.

Most of the platypuses limped heavily, bills low and knuckles dragging. The geckos had stopped interrupting each other. The young possums clung to their parents in silent despair, and the trapdoor spiders trembled under the burning sun.

The frogs looked worst of all. Cracked skin, torn feet, eyes reddened from whipping sand. And they kept checking the watery boxes where the tadpoles lived. Pigo stayed away from the tadpoles, because he didn't want to scare them—but he edged near enough to hear the old frog called Jir telling Darel, "If we don't find water by tomorrow, they're not going to make it."

"We will find water," Darel promised Old Jir, his heart breaking at the sight of the overheated tadpoles curled together in a shrinking puddle. "I'm sure of it."

But as the dunes turned to hard-packed sand, he didn't smell the faintest whiff of moisture in the biting air. Still, the refugees staggered through the merciless desert. When the broiling sun finally dipped below the horizon, the air cooled, and Darel pushed onward toward the shelter of a clump of red rocks.

A lone tree rose from the scrub farther on, but Darel knew the outback a little better now. "Farther on" meant a half day's trek . . . and the tadpoles wouldn't last that long.

After the refugees reached the red rocks, Darel looked after everyone as well as he could, then slumped to the dirt in an exhausted sleep.

When he awoke, Pigo and the scorpions were gone.

Darel didn't say anything. He just stood and stared at the place where they'd been. He looked at all the abandoned stretchers with nobody to pull them, at Old Jir barely breathing, and at Ponto still wrapped in a spiderweb body cast. At all the wounded creatures, clinging to life, who'd followed him into battle—and into this terrible land.

His eyes burned and he wanted to cry, but he was too dry to make tears.

As the camp roused, Gee hopped up beside Darel and sat in silence. Then Coorah did the same. Quoba and Burnu joined them next, then Pippi's sister waddled over, with Effie crawling beside her.

Nobody spoke for a long time.

Then Dingo croaked, from the top of the red rocks, "Hey, why did the scorpion cross the desert—"

"Nobody's in the mood for jokes," Burnu snapped at her.

"—dragging logs?"

"What?"

"The scorpions." Dingo pointed toward the lone tree off in the distance. "They're coming back with firewood."

Darel jumped to his feet, shaded his eyes from the morning glare, and caught sight of Pigo leading his scorpions closer. "Are those branches?"

"Definitely logs," Dingo said.

"Why logs?" Coorah asked.

"To get to the other side," Dingo said.

Nobody laughed. Not even Dingo. Instead, they stared in silence as Pigo and his scorpions came closer and closer.

"They're roots," Pigo announced when he reached the rocks. "Of the mallee eucalyptus."

"You marched the entire night," Effie asked, her spider eyes dubious, "for a bunch of roots?"

Pigo hefted a long, gnarled root onto his shoulder. "We hacked them from the ground with our pincers."

"What are they for?" Darel asked.

"This," Pigo said, striking forward.

He tilted the root over a tadpole bassinet like he

was going to smash it. Frogs gasped in fear—then *water* flowed from inside the root, and filled the bassinet. The scent of fresh, clean, cool liquid struck Darel where he stood. Other scorps filled the rest of the bassinets, then passed around the remaining roots. Enough was left for one sprinkle per frog, one lick per gecko, and one sip for everyone else.

Enough to keep them alive for another day.

34

THE SUN BEAT DOWN, STRETCHING THE minutes into hours, and the hours into a painful, stumbling daze. The refugees dragged themselves past withered bushes and lifeless plains, too weary to raise their heads when scouts located a dry spring in a patch of dead trees.

"On the same straight line," Darel said to himself. "Still following the underground river."

Nobody listened. Nobody cared. They just kept struggling across the dry scrub . . . until a strange shape rose from the farthest dunes.

"What's that?" Gee mumbled, tugging a platypus's stretcher with Darel. "Looks like a—"

"A red moon," Effie said, dragging a stretcher beside them. "Peeking over the horizon."

"There's only one moon." Gee snorted weakly. "Silly spider."

"I didn't say it was a moon. I said it *looked* like—"

"It's a rock." Darel stopped. "It's a rock tower. And I've seen it before."

"I'm pretty sure that if you'd been here before," Gee told him, "you would've mentioned it."

For a long moment, Darel simply stared at the distant rock, remembering his dream of a rainbow arching over a red tower. Then he cleared his throat and croaked, "Listen up!"

A handful of frogs and platypuses looked at him, but everyone else kept dragging themselves along, heads bowed and shoulders slumped.

"Attention!" Pigo roared, snapping his pincer. "The king speaks!"

With slow shuffles and pained sighs, the rest of the refugees turned toward Darel.

"I've seen that before!" Darel called out, pointing to the red rock tower. "The Rainbow Serpent showed me that in a dream. We're almost there! We're almost home! Head for the rock!"

A ragged cheer sounded, and the refugees trekked onward with renewed determination. They walked for hours, and at midday they reached the immense shadow that the rocky tower cast across the scrub. There was still no scent of water, but at least the shade gave the refugees just enough strength to continue moving.

Darel marched ahead of the others, desperate for a whiff of dampness in the air. Except, as the sun lowered toward the dunes, he smelled nothing but drought.

Finally, the refugees arrived at the base of the rock tower, and Effie stared in awe and whispered, "The whole thing is one rock. A single rock sticking up from underground."

"Not from underground," Quoba told her.

Darel looked closer, and a bubble of wonder expanded in his chest. The tower didn't rise from the flat desert. Instead, it stood upright on a mound of boulders: huge round stones directly beneath the tower, then smaller boulders scattered around the edges.

Most of the refugees stared in awe, but a few of the geckos scampered toward the boulders.

"Cool!" a gecko crackled.

"Shade!"

"Don't tip the whole thing over!" Effie warned. "Are those rocks steady or—"

"Sturdy as a stump!" another gecko said from the space between boulders.

"Not going anywhere!" the first said.

"Well," Effie said, "can you find any—"

"No water!" a third gecko reported. "Not inside."

Coorah stepped up beside Darel, her eyes bulging at the tower. "It's amazing," she breathed. "It's impossible."

"It's *dry*," Gee told her. "Unless we can drink rock, we're in trouble."

The bubble of wonder in Darel's chest popped and was replaced by dread. They weren't just in trouble. Without water, they were dead. Every platypus, every tadpole, everyone. Dead.

"I don't—" He blinked his tearless eyes. "I don't understand."

"The good news," Dingo said, craning her head to look upward, "is that this thing makes an awesome gravestone."

"I don't understand!" Darel repeated, almost wailing. "The underground rivers all lead here. You saw that! The Rainbow Serpent told me—my father drew tunnels in the cave paintings! I *can't* be wrong!" He fell to his knees. "There's water here, there has to be . . ."

"I don't smell any," Gee said gently.

"Then I did all this for *nothing*? I helped Marmoo invade? I helped him kill the Amphibilands." Darel choked on a sob. "I dragged wounded soldiers, dying friends—tadpoles!—across the desert. I trusted the Rainbow Serpent all for nothing?"

"Not for nothing," an eerie voice whispered from above. *"Dragging across the desert gave us time—"*

"Ghost bats!" Gee shouted. "Watch out!"

"—to get reinforcements."

A legion of ghost bats swarmed around the massive rock tower and dove toward the refugees. Half of the bats gripped black pebbles in their claws, and for a second, Darel didn't understand. Pebbles wouldn't do much damage.

Then the bats opened their claws to drop the pebbles—and Darel gasped.

They weren't pebbles. They were paralysis ticks.

PIPPI CLAWED MUD FROM THE BURROW wall, then wriggled her bill back and forth in the dirt. Nothing. She smacked her dry mouth and clawed more mud. Still nothing. She dug deeper and deeper until she felt a faint tingle—then she lunged forward and grabbed a beetle in her mouth.

"Took wong enuff," she mumbled, keeping a firm grip on a wriggling leg.

After a full day of searching, she'd only found two beetles, and neither of them was juicy. She sighed. Platypuses were no good at hunting in the mud. She needed a river.

But the river was gone.

In the main chamber, she plopped the beetle in front of a dozing Yabber. "Dinner time, Yabber!" she said, trying to sound cheerful.

One of his eyes opened. "I just ate."

"That was this morning. It's dinner now."

"When's the last time *you* ate?"

"Breakfast," she lied. "I'm still packed."

"When's the last time you had a real drink of water?"

"Uh . . ." She'd been weak from thirst for so long that she couldn't remember. "I soaked plenty from the dripping wall. And we need *you* to get stronger, so you can dreamcast us out of here."

"Just a few more days," he told her. "I mean to say, that nightcasting almost killed me. I'm still weak. But once I—"

Crrrrrrg! The burrow walls gave a violent shudder. The floor quaked, the roof shook, and clumps of dirt thudded around Pippi and pelted Yabber's shell.

"Cave-in!" Pippi yelped, steadying herself. "C'mon, c'mon—outside!"

She tugged Yabber toward the door, clawed through mud, and shoved him through the doorway. As the walls collapsed completely, she lunged from the burrow and tumbled to the dry riverbank, where she bonked painfully into Yabber's shell.

Then she saw them. A dozen scorpions standing directly over her burrow, lashing at the ground with their stingers. Making the earth shake, making the walls cave in.

Pippi whimpered . . . and another squad of scorpions surrounded her.

"You can't hide, you duck-faced freak," Marmoo snarled, shoving through his scorps. "Not from me. I own every leaf and ditch in the Arachnilands, and soon I'll own the entire outback." His melted mouthparts shifted into a horrible smile. "Water. You think water is the key to life?"

Pippi gulped and trembled.

"Do you?" Marmoo roared.

"Y-y-yes?"

"It's also the key to *death*." Marmoo turned and glared at his squad. "Bring them! And if the turtle starts to dreamcast, sting the platypus!"

Two scorpions grabbed Pippi with sharp-edged pincers, and she was so scared that she almost fainted. She panted and shivered as the scorpions dragged her and Yabber along the reeking riverbank, past smoldering fire pits and clear-cut woods.

When the scorps finally shoved her around a weedy corner, her eyes widened. A massive dam stretched across the dry river directly in front of her. It was built of thick logs lashed together with ropes and vines and spider silk. It was even larger than she'd thought, and it creaked as water lapped against the other side.

"No," Yabber gasped, then turned to look at Marmoo. "What are you doing?"

Marmoo backhanded Yabber with a pincer, flinging him shell over heels. "Whatever I want."

Yabber hit the ground with a thud, and Pippi yelped "Hey!" a second before the scorps shoved her after him.

"What *is* this?" Yabber asked.

"It's the dam," she said. "Like I told you."

"There's a reason the frogs never built dams." Yabber angled his long neck toward Marmoo. "The Veil may have drawn too much water here, but . . . the intention was never to hoard it. Because water is life. Water is free. You can't block—"

"Water is *mine*!" Marmoo roared, kicking Yabber with his forelegs.

The crack of the blow rang out, and Yabber was hurled into the air, spinning wildly. He slammed into the dam wall, then slumped to the ground with a groan, dazed and wheezing.

Marmoo scuttled closer, his stinger raised to strike.

36

S THE GHOST BATS SWARMED CLOSER, Darel reached for his dagger—then froze. He didn't want to fight them; he didn't want any more bloodshed.

"Wait!" he shouted. "Stop!"

"*Reinforcements,*" a red-eyed bat whispered, swooping at him. "*We warned you.*"

"*Emperor Marmoo said you've suffered enough—*"

"—*and now we can feed,*" another bat hissed before sinking her fangs into Pirra's tail.

Pirra shrieked, the red-eyed bat slashed Darel's arm, and a cluster of bats landed on the still-unconscious Ponto. The *pock-pock* of falling ticks sounded around Darel as bats flickered toward fleeing geckos and wrapped trapdoor spiders in leathery white wings.

"Scorpions, guard the tadpoles!" Darel yelled, vaulting upward and swinging his dagger. "Archers, fire!"

"Geckos!" Coorah shouted, pegging a bat with her slingshot. "Hide in the rocks!"

Darel parried the red-eyed bat's claws in the air. "Platypuses, close ranks and get your spurs up!"

"*Ch-ch.*" The ticks crept closer. "*Ch*-time to feed-*ch*, suck the blood."

"Possums!" Gee bellowed, jumping past Darel and clubbing the red-eyed bat. "You know what to do!"

The possums keeled over as Darel landed on a tick that was crawling toward the triplets. "Frogs," he shouted. "Attack!"

"Kulipari!" a frog with cracked skin and swollen eyes shouted, grabbing a stone for a weapon.

Another frog raised her crutch like a spear. "Kulipari!"

A white-lipped tree frog caught a bat's wing with her tongue, and three burrowing frogs heaved themselves from stretchers to fight, while Darel's mom guarded the bassinets and the triplets collected rocks as ammunition behind her.

But many of the frogs barely moved. They were too weak.

"*They're dying of thirst,*" one of the bats hissed. "*Easy targets for our— Aah!*"

Dingo's bow slugged the bat. "Did someone say 'Kulipari'?" she asked, spinning her bow into a blur, smashing ticks left and right.

"Don't tap your poison!" Old Jir called from his stretcher. "You're too drained—all of you!"

"In that case—" Burnu jumped onto Pigo's tail and hurled his boomerangs. "Frog toss!"

Pigo snapped his tail, launching Burnu into the thick of the ghost bats as spiderwebs flashed past.

Burnu twisted like a tornado, shredding the bat swarm. On the rock tower behind him, Quoba held one fighting stick in each hand . . . and launched at the ghost bats fleeing from Burnu, her sticks flinging them in every direction.

Then Burnu landed—on his face. Frozen into a bizarre position by three tick bites on his back.

"*Ch*-amphiblood!" the ticks chittered. "*Ch-ch*, tasty."

"Get those off him!" Darel shouted, smashing another tick. "Someone, quick!"

"Don't bother," Burnu slurred, his face on the ground. "I'll handle it."

His eyes darkened and he started to glow faintly.

"Burnu, no!" Old Jir yelled. "If you tap your poison, you're dead!"

"If I don't," Burnu mumbled, "we're *all* dead."

A hail of rocks slammed into him, smashing the paralysis ticks. The triplets cheered from behind Darel's mom . . . then they saw that one of the rocks they'd thrown had knocked Burnu out.

"Oops," Tipi said.

Dingo leaped up beside Burnu, twirling her bow to protect him, just as Darel swerved toward Pigo. He landed in front of the big scorpion, directly between his pincers, and bashed the ticks on the ground while Pigo's pincers flashed above him, taking out ghost bats.

For a long moment, neither spoke. They just grunted and struck, fighting together with a deadly precision.

"We're a good team," Darel panted.

Pigo grunted. "It's an honor to die in your service," he said gruffly.

"Well, that's not very cheerful—"

Darel heard a *ch-ch-ch* and realized that Pigo's pincers weren't moving anymore. They were frozen in place, and ticks were swarming across his carapace—and leaping directly at him.

With a flash of panic, Darel spun away. But he

was too slow. A tick bit his knee, and he collapsed onto his side.

The world tilted, his vision turning everything sideways. He saw the ticks on Dingo's arms sideways, as ghost bats enveloped her. He saw the triplets sideways as they fled from ticks. He saw Coorah and Pirra and the bullfrogs and spiders and scorps sideways, all paralyzed and motionless.

Darel scrabbled against the red earth with his good leg, squirming toward his mom and siblings an inch at a time. It couldn't end like this. Not after they'd come so far.

Then Quoba bounded from the boulders, and Darel felt a spark of hope. He heard the slash of her fighting sticks, and the enraged hissing of bats. Then she flashed into view, frozen in a crouch—paralyzed in the middle of a jump—and smashed into the rock tower.

Darel winced as she plummeted, hit the boulders, and bounced a few times. Then only Gee still fought, using a whip to slash at the ticks swarming Pigo. The ticks fled, and Gee leaped after them, cracking his whip.

Except it wasn't a whip.

"Eat possum, ghosties!" Gee screamed, holding

the burly possum's arms and snapping his tail into the air.

Two ghost bats flopped to the ground . . . but a third one slammed Gee from behind, and a wrinkled tick jumped on him.

"*Ch! Ch!*" The wrinkled tick jabbed its piercing mouthparts into Gee's shoulder. "Jui*ch*iest frog ever!"

Only a dozen ghost bats remained airborne, but a tide of ticks still poured toward the frozen refugees. "Warm *ch*-blood," they chittered. "Fresh *ch*-blood."

Then a green light sparked near the rock tower, and Quoba slowly stood, her eyes turning black.

"No," Darel whispered. "You'll burn out."

She smiled faintly, then glowed brighter—and rocketed at the ghost bats in an emerald blur. When she landed, the bats were gone, but her skin had turned a pale green, and her glow was fading fast. Still, she turned toward the ticks and tapped her poison again. So deeply that the blackness in her eyes seemed to spread to her face.

"Don't!" Darel called. "No, Quoba!"

She saluted him with one of her fighting sticks and leaped at the ticks, tapping even deeper into her poison.

Tears swam in Darel's eyes. He couldn't watch Quoba destroy herself. He couldn't watch his family and friends slaughtered at the end of the world. But there was nothing he could do to stop it.

37

DAREL BLINKED HIS INNER EYELIDS AND stared hopelessly at the rock tower. Afraid to look at Quoba's last stand. Despair filled him. Fear, anger, defeat, and helplessness. Then the tears finally started . . .

And he gasped. "*No way*: the blob . . ."

With his tear-blurred, sideways vision, the rocky tower looked exactly like the "blob" in the cave painting in the Snowy Mountains! This was the place. Not just from his dream, but from his father's cave paintings. The Rainbow Serpent *had* led him here for a reason. Except, why was the rock standing upright, instead of lying on its side?

"The underground rivers all point here," he said. "But what about that frog below the blob? The frog with a pointy tail . . ."

He crawled one-legged toward the boulders, scraping his skin against the pebbled ground. When he reached the lowest boulders, he pulled himself upright with his finger pads and glanced behind him.

Everything was still. The slumped forms of bats and ticks dotted the ground—and Quoba, hunched beside the tadpoles, her head bowed. Alive but pale, fishbelly-white like Old Jir. She'd never use her power again.

She'd sacrificed herself, just the way his father had.

Darel clenched his jaw. He wasn't going to fail her, not now. He wasn't going to fail any of them. He dragged himself higher across the mound of boulders, crawling feebly toward the base of the rocky tower.

Then he stopped. "The tower's on the boulders. So if I move the boulders . . ."

The tower would fall. Sideways. Exactly like the "blob" in the cave painting. So he needed to shift the boulders—but how?

He crawled from boulder to boulder, running his finger pads over every crack and crevice. His world shrank to the length of his arms and the rasp of rough stone on his skin. First he checked the biggest boulders, directly beneath the tower. Massive, mighty rocks that might hold massive, mighty secrets. He found nothing. He checked the medium-size rocks next, and still found nothing.

Finally, the weight of failure heavy on his heart, he

checked the smallest rocks crammed together at the base of the mound of boulders. Boring little nothing rocks . . . until his probing finger pads touched a slit in a stone.

A small slit in a small boulder, wedged under a few middle-size boulders, which supported one massive one.

He tried to shove the small boulder. It didn't budge. He leaned back and kicked with his good leg, but the rock still didn't budge. It was jammed in too tight.

Darel looked closer. Except for the slit, it was an ordinary rock. Boring and useless—like the wood frog of rocks. Nothing special, not weighty, not powerful.

Ordinary frogs have power, too, the turtle king said, in Darel's memory.

"Maybe ordinary *frogs* do," Darel grumbled. "But not ordinary *rocks*."

How could a boring little rock topple a stone tower the size of a mountain? Not possible. No way.

Except . . . the Rainbow Serpent hadn't chosen an extraordinary frog like Burnu or Quoba or even Chief Olba. The Rainbow Serpent had chosen *him*, an ordinary wood frog. So maybe the biggest changes started with the littlest things.

"And that frog looked ordinary," he said to himself.

"That pointy frog in the cave painting wasn't special except for—"

Darel bit his lip. *Except for the pointy thing.* Maybe it wasn't a tail; maybe it was a weapon—a blade. He pulled the dagger from his belt, and the reflection of sunlight against the red rock tower glinted on the blade.

Like a rainbow.

Darel closed his eyes. *This is for Arabanoo. For Pippi and Yabber. For King Sergu and Chief Olba and Princess Orani. For all the fallen frogs and platypuses. For the possums and geckos and trapdoor spiders. For the harrier hawks and the land crayfish, wherever they are. And for the scorpions, too.*

"Takes all kinds," he said. "And one in the hand *is* worth two in the bush."

Then he slid his dagger into the slit in the rock.

38

NOTHING HAPPENED.

Darel looked at the huge rock tower. He looked at the boulders, then at his dagger, buried to the hilt in the small rock.

"Come on," he said.

He jiggled the hilt. Nothing happened. Then he turned the dagger like a key . . . and the rock shifted! He just needed leverage to move the rock away from the bigger rocks on top. Bracing his leg, he turned the hilt harder . . . and—*grrrrrrrrch!*—the rock popped from the pile and rolled away.

"Ha!" Darel said. "Gotcha!"

Crrrrrrgghhhhh! The bigger boulders shifted with a grating roar like a mountain clearing its throat.

"Jump!" Gee screamed. "You wart-head, jump!"

"Avalanche!" Pirra yelled, while Effie chittered something about it looking like a trapdoor.

"Darel!" his mom called. "Watch out!"

"Crazy mud frog," Burnu muttered as Pigo barked, "Retreat, my king!"

Darel's eyes bulged when he saw the entire ragtag army of refugees watching him.

Well, watching him and *shouting* at him.

Darel hopped onto one foot and leaped away as the rock mound collapsed in a landslide. Boulders tumbled and crashed together, sending rock chips flying. Inches ahead of the avalanche, Darel raced desperately on one leg, his other still frozen from the tick bite. He lost his balance, caught himself, and finally leaped sideways toward the others.

He slammed to the ground beside Gee as the roaring wave of rocks churned past. Pain flared in his leg and his side—and the biggest rocks, the massive, mighty ones at the base of the tower, suddenly gave way.

The tower tilted.

Slowly at first, leaning lower as the earth trembled and the howl of grinding rocks filled the air. The tower crushed boulder after boulder, and Gee and Coorah leaped onto Darel to protect him, and . . . *SLAM*.

The tower fell with a crash that rang in Darel's ears. The ground heaved and wind blasted red sand across the scrubland. In the far distance, from the direction of the Amphibilands, a bright light shone straight upward, reaching to the stars.

"What is it?" Pigo asked, his voice soft with awe.

Darel blinked against the plumes of red dust, but before he could say a word, a shudder passed through Pigo and the scorpions. Then the spiders, the Kulipari, and the platypuses turned toward the Amphibilands. Everyone with poison gazed at the glow of the majestic pillar of light.

Even Quoba, no longer poisonous, and Old Jir, who'd burned through his power years ago, seemed caught by the distant light.

Then Darel's breath caught. Because Old Jir's eyes started to glow. Not the midnight black of a Kulipari, but a brilliant white. The kind of white that follows fire.

Darel didn't understand—and a moment later, the light faded in the distance, followed by the glow of the old frog's eyes.

"The Scrolls," Jir whispered.

Nobody spoke. Nobody moved. And that's when Darel heard it: the first, faint gurgle of water.

Through her tears, Pippi watched Marmoo raise his stinger to strike.

"No!" she yelped, her bill curled in terror.

Marmoo's stinger stopped an inch from Yabber's neck. "You want me to sting you first?" he asked her.

"Please, no—"

"You're weak! Born in ponds and rivers!" His tail quivered. "Soft like water, not hard like rock, not—"

A *glug* sounded, and Marmoo swiveled his ruined face toward the dam.

Glug. Glug-glug.

"Soft," Yabber murmured, "is not the same as weak . . ."

"Report in!" Marmoo bellowed to his troops atop the dam. "What's happening?"

GLUG. GLUG-GLUG.

"The water, Emperor Marmoo!" a scorp called down. "It's swirling in a circle, like . . . a drain!"

"Draining?" Marmoo raged. "*My* water is draining away?"

The dam creaked and crackled behind Pippi, and water seeped between the lashed-together trees. *Creak . . .*

"The waves are bashing the dams!" the scorp yelled. "They—"

A distant *crack* echoed across the Amphibilands, followed by the roar of water. *Glug! Glug, glug, glug-glug.*

"A dam's breaking!" another scorp screamed. "Emperor, the water's free, it's—"

"It's mine!" Marmoo roared, slashing at the dam in a fury, stabbing holes in the logs with his stinger. "Mine!"

Pippi dove toward Yabber an instant before the dam broke. Webbing tore and vines snapped, and then the huge tree trunks shattered, whipping chunks of wood through the air. Scorpions screamed and water glugged, and in the distance more dam walls cracked.

"Stand and fight!" Marmoo bellowed, slashing at a tree trunk. "Kill! Conquer!"

For a single heartbeat, Pippi crouched beside the protection of Yabber's shell—then the tidal wave hit. The first gush lifted her and Yabber like a huge watery hand, then slammed Marmoo in the thorax and swept him away.

The shrieks of the scorpions grew panicked and desperate, but the pounding wave of cool, clean water felt like home to Pippi. She rode the onrushing flow as scorpions and spiders thrashed and tumbled in terror.

She sped halfway across the Amphibilands in that first surge of water, keeping Yabber close, dodging legions of submerged scorps. Marmoo's entire horde was being swept away by the water.

Pippi swam for the surface, pulling Yabber with her, and gulped a breath of air.

"Well, *that* was unexpected," Yabber said, his eyes opening.

"You didn't do it?" Pippi asked.

"I didn't do a single thing, I'm ashamed to admit." He straightened his neck, looking ahead of them.

"Oh, my."

Just around the bend, three rivers crashed together, sending great plumes of spray into the air above a huge whirlpool. The water spun with tremendous force, churning with froth and debris . . . and Marmoo.

His legs flailing and his pincers snapping, the scorpion lord lashed at the water, but the water didn't care. The whirlpool flung him in tighter and tighter circles, faster and faster, deeper and deeper. He screamed, he raged, he battered the current with blows that no enemy could survive . . . and then the water dragged him under.

As the current drove Pippi forward, a glimmer of golden light shone around Yabber's flipper. He pointed toward the spot where Marmoo had disappeared, and a moment later the enraged scorpion

lord rose above the water, suspended in a dreamcast bubble.

"What are you doing?" Pippi shouted. "Don't save him!"

"Life is a gift from the Rainbow Serpent," Yabber told her. "All life, even *his*. We must cherish this gift, and protect it."

"You did this!" Marmoo screamed, his scarred side eyes gleaming when he spotted Yabber. "I'll tear you from your shell! I'll hunt down every frog and destroy them one by one! I'll burn your hatchlings to ashes!"

Yabber's face changed, until he looked cold and hard, as if he'd been carved from stone. "But sometimes, protecting life requires sacrifice."

He dropped his flipper and the golden glow vanished.

Marmoo plunged back underwater. Waves frothed where the scorpion lord's tail thrashed. His mouthparts opened in a silent scream. His pincers snapped and his legs churned fast and hard. Then his tail went limp, and his legs kicked slower and weaker. Until, finally, he stopped moving altogether.

Marmoo had found the one thing he couldn't defeat.

"Take a deep breath," Yabber told Pippi. "We're going in."

Pippi looked at the whirlpool. "In *that*? After what just happened to *him*?"

"Marmoo fought the water, and died." Yabber arched his neck. "We'll ride the water, and live."

"How far down does it go?"

"We're about to find out!"

"What if we run out of air?" she shouted as the current dragged them to the edge of the whirlpool.

Yabber looped his neck toward her, and his eyes glowed golden. "We won't."

The current whipped Pippi sideways, then tossed her in a circle—around and around as Marmoo's limp form tumbled past.

Then the whirlpool dragged her under.

39

ED DUST FILLED DAREL'S VISION. He heard the liquid gurgle change to a trickle—and then the trickle change to a gush. The sound reminded him of water rushing through reed pipes after turning a spigot.

The idea caught fire in his mind. *A spigot. A faucet.* That was it! The huge red rock acted as a valve! When he'd knocked the rock tower down, he'd turned on a massive spigot. With the help of the Rainbow Serpent's magic, he'd triggered the underground tunnels that crossed the outback from here to the watery Amphibilands. Tunnels that acted like enormous reed pipes, filling with gushing, pouring, flowing—

"*Water!*" Effie shouted joyfully. "Water, look!"

"Seeping around the rock!" another trapdoor spider said.

"Seeping around the *everywhere*!" Effie announced, laughing.

"All I can see is red dust," Gee grumbled.

Effie chittered. "Silly frog-eyes!"

"She's right!" Pigo said, alarmed. "Watch out—there's *water* coming from the ground!"

"Scorpions!" Darel called, grinning at the worry in Pigo's voice. "Follow my voice, onto the rock!"

"Fall in!" Pigo barked. "Follow the Blue Sky King to dry land!"

Darel took a step, and his leg buckled. "Maybe not my best idea ever."

"You've had worse ones," Coorah said, laughing. "But can you smell that, Darel? Water. Fresh, cool water!"

Excited croaks sounded through the dust, along with shrieks of glee: "Ooh! Water! Look at me, I'm all wet! Drink up!"

"Follow the king, scorpions!" Effie said, lifting Darel onto a silken-web hammock.

He croaked in surprise, then called, "Scorpions, this way! Watch out for the rocks! Now climb the webbing to the top."

Effie and a few other spiders carried Darel higher and higher, until he emerged in dust-free air. Even on its side, the red rock tower loomed over the bleak, harsh outback that spread endlessly in all directions.

Lifeless. Dead. Hostile.

Except, when the dust settled, the landscape changed. Water bubbled and frothed around the red rock, and a pond welled up from underground. Not a pond, a *lake*. Dozens of streams flowed from the lake, surging across the dry, cracked earth. A geyser rose from the middle, shooting sprays and jets in every direction, splashing and splattering into a pure white mist.

Darel stepped from Effie's hammock, his eyes bulging with wonder.

When the sun shone on the mist, rainbows formed. Not one, not two, but *hundreds* of little rainbows arched through the vapor, and where they touched the thirsty earth, plants grew. Tiny buds that unfurled into delicate seedlings.

Saplings rose, with branches spreading and newborn leaves trembling, becoming trees before his eyes. Not fully grown yet, but a start of something. This wasn't simply water flowing across the outback. It was a new land.

"The Rainbow Serpent," Darel whispered.

Down below the red rock, frogs leaped and laughed and swam, possums splashed, and platypuses waded into the refreshing coolness. Tadpoles flashed in the shallows, racing each other around the legs of thirsty trapdoor spiders.

Colors shimmered in the pools of water rippling from the lake, and a gleam of purple and black caught Darel's eyes. His father's colors. "Dad," he said.

His mother must've seen the same shimmer, because she stepped up beside him and said, "Your father would be so proud."

"He's not the only one," Burnu told Darel from where Coorah was bandaging his head. "We all are."

Darel bowed his head to hide his smile . . . and saw Quoba standing in the still-growing lake with Old Jir, two white splotches against the blue. His smile faded at the sight of her pale skin. No more poison. No more power.

"Even Quoba," Burnu told him. "*Especially* her. You made her sacrifice worthwhile."

"D-d-do you really think so?"

"He *knows* so," Ponto said from his stretcher behind Darel.

Darel spun, his throat inflating in relief. "You're finally awake!"

"I'm in a spiderweb," Ponto grunted, eyeing his silken body cast. "And there aren't even any flies."

"That reminds me!" Dingo stumbled closer, stiff

from tick bites. "Did you hear what one spider said to the other?"

"Which spider?" Ponto asked with a worried frown. "What'd they say?"

"'Time's fun when you're having flies!'"

Ponto scowled at the bad joke, and everyone else groaned. Gee, Coorah, Nioka, all the spiders and geckos—even the triplets—groaned. All except the scorpions. Pigo and his scorpions laughed and laughed, nudging each other and saying, "Get it? Get it? *Time's* fun *when you're having* flies!"

"Finally!" Dingo high-fived a scorpion's tail. "Someone who appreciates high-quality humor!"

"Just when I was learning to like scorps, too," Burnu said.

Darel grinned at him as playful splashes and happy shouts rose from the lake below. Then the shouts turned to alarm.

"You've got to see this," Gee called from the edge of the rock.

Darel hopped closer and inflated his throat in surprise. The geyser still bubbled up in the center of the lake—but now it was *glowing*.

"What is *that*?" Coorah asked.

"That," Darel said, recognizing the golden color, "is Yabber."

A second later, a golden bubble burst from the depths, splashed onto the lake's surface, and popped, revealing Yabber, his eyes shining like the sun—and Pippi, her eyes shining with excitement.

"*Wooooooo-hoooooo!*" she shouted, then slapped her tail in joy when she saw her family. "Pirra! Mom! Dad!"

"And Pippi," Darel breathed.

Gee jumped up and down beside him. "Pippi! It's Pippi! Pippi's back!"

While Pippi hugged her family, Yabber's eyes dimmed and he looped his neck from one side to the other, looking at all the creatures, the lake and streams, the budding plants. Finally, he turned toward the rock, then tilted his head higher and higher until he met Darel's face.

Yabber said something Darel couldn't hear.

A moment later, the frogs and platypuses in the lake all turned toward Darel. The possums on the shore gazed at him, and the burrowing frogs and trapdoor spiders looked up from the holes they'd been digging in the water-softened soil.

Darel bulged his eyes toward Quoba and mouthed, "What? What now?"

She smiled, lifted her pale arm, and pointed at him. No. She pointed *behind* him.

When Darel turned, his breath caught. A rainbow stretched across the sky above the great red rock. And like water welling up from the parched earth, Darel felt the rise of peace in his heart.

Days passed, days of healing and hope and also of hard work. One night, Darel sat alone at a campfire on the shore of the lake. The fire flickered merrily, and the heat soothed his aches and pains. The crackle of the flames mixed with the laughter of the young ones still splashing in the water.

At another campfire, his mother chatted with Nioka and one of the trapdoor spider mothers, trading stories and making plans. It was the sound of a new future being born.

Darel smiled and stoked the fire with his dagger. Sparks twirled and rose in the smoke.

"What are you seeing?" Old Jir asked, sitting beside him.

"Nothing," he said. "Just sparks."

The old Kulipari looked at him. "Where you

see sparks, I see a miracle. So we're seeing the same thing."

Darel ducked his head. In the past few days, he'd heard enough gratitude to last a lifetime. Just remembering all the praise made his face heat with embarrassment. It was different coming from Jir, though, because the old frog knew all of Darel's doubts and fears and failures.

"Thanks," he said, stirring the embers again.

After a time, Old Jir took the dagger from Darel's hand. "Your father's weapon. It was more powerful than we ever expected."

"It saved us."

"*You* saved us."

As Old Jir scratched shapes in the dirt with the dagger, a soft chorus of night frogs started up across the lake. Soon the possums and geckos joined in, a gentle song of hope. "Do you know where your father got this dagger?" he asked, sketching more lines on the ground.

"Sure," Darel told him, studying the marks in the dirt: a picture of a frog skeleton, some sort of insignia. "I've heard that story a hundred times."

Old Jir lifted his head, his eyes gleaming in the firelight. "Not the whole story. Not the *real* story."

"You mean . . ." Darel's heart beat faster at the expression on the old warrior's face. "There's more?"

"Much more," Old Jir said with a sharp nod. "If you want to hear it."

Darel leaned forward. "Yes."

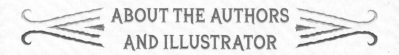

ABOUT THE AUTHORS AND ILLUSTRATOR

TREVOR PRYCE is a retired NFL player and writer who's written for the *New York Times* and NBC.com. He's also developed television and movie scripts for Sony Pictures, Cartoon Network, Disney, ABC, and HBO, among others. He lives in Maryland.

JOEL NAFTALI is the author of many books, several written with his wife, Lee. He lives in California.

SANFORD GREENE is an accomplished comics illustrator whose work has been published by Marvel, DC Comics, Disney, Nickelodeon, Dark Horse, and more. He lives in South Carolina.